D1151440

SLOW DRVR

Books by Tristan Bancks

My Life & Other Stuff I Made Up

My Life & Other Stuff that Went Wrong

My Life & Other Massive Mistakes

My Life & Other Exploding Chickens

Two Wolves

The Fall (May 2017)

Mac Slater, Coolhunter

Mac Slater, Imaginator

Tristan Bancks

pics by gus gordon

RANDOM HOUSE AUSTRALIA

A Random House book
Published by Penguin Random House Australia Pty Ltd
Level 3, 100 Pacific Highway, North Sydney NSW 2060
www.penguin.com.au

First published by Random House Australia in 2017

Addresses for the Penguin Random House group of companies can be found at global.penguinrandomhouse.com/offices.

National Library of Australia
Cataloguing-in-Publication entry

Creator: Bancks, Tristan, author
Title: My life and other weaponised muffins/Tristan Bancks; Gus Gordon
ISBN: 9780143781066 (paperback)
Series: Bancks, Tristan My life; 5
Target Audience: For primary school age
Subjects: Children's stories
Other Creators/Contributors: Gordon, Gus, illustrator

Cover and internal illustrations by Gus Gordon
Cover and internal design by Astred Hicks, designcherry
Printed in Australia by Griffin Press, an accredited ISO AS/NZS 14001:2004 Environmental Management System printer

Penguin Random House Australia uses papers that are natural, renewable and recyclable products and made from wood grown in sustainable forests. The logging and manufacturing processes are expected to conform to the environmental regulations of the country of origin.

Contents

Hey,
I'm Tom Weekly, and this is my fifth book of freaky, funny short stories about my life.

Eating is pretty much my favourite sport – Mum reckons I demolish the week's shopping in one afternoon – and almost every story in this book features food: flying meatballs, melted Bubble O' Bills, Australia's stickiest toffee, a very special chocolate mousse, rat's tail French fries, weaponised muffins and the world's tastiest toenails.

As well as sharing these mouth-watering treats, I'll answer some of the toughest questions facing the youth of today:

1. What should you do if you're at a friend's house for dinner and you find a very long, very thick hair in your meal?

2. How many spiders would you need to have crawling on your body for 30 seconds in order to beat the Guinness World Record?

3. What's an ingenious way to get out of Friday morning's maths test?

4. What do you do if you're trapped alone in a runaway car, speeding backwards downhill, and you can't find the brakes?

5. How can you turn a friend's incurable head lice problem into a profitable business?

There's a wise, ancient saying that I like to quote: 'Sometimes life can give you an atomic wedgie. Don't even bother to pick it out.'

Stay weird.

Tom

Meatball

Jack's mum makes the best meatballs in the world. They are delicious and delumptious. If there were a meatball Olympics, Mrs Danalis would win gold. I always manage to score an invitation to Jack's house on meatball night. I've eaten 17 of those little nuggets of heaven so far. I have one left on my plate and – I can't believe I'm saying this – there's no way I'm eating it.

'Go on,' Mrs D says. 'Don't be polite.'

I glance around the table. They're watching me. Mrs Danalis, Mr Danalis, Jack and his rotten little three-year-old brother, Barney, have all finished their meals. Mrs D has a rule that no one leaves the table and there's no dessert until everyone is done.

'Eat up, Tom, and I'll serve the tiramisu,' she says.

My mouth gushes with saliva and my stomach licks its lips at the mention of Mrs D's tiramisu – a creamy, cakey Italian dessert.

It's my second favourite food in the world.

'Move it along, mate,' says Mr D. 'Game starts in five minutes.'

'Yeah, hurry up, you big boobyman!' Barney screeches, then throws his head back, laughing like crazy.

'Don't say "boobyman" at the dinner table, please, Barney,' says Mr D.

'*You* just said it!' Barney replies, then he laughs again and sings, 'Booo-by-man, booo-by-man, booo-by-man!'

Barney has been voted Australia's most annoying child three years in a row.

'We'll ignore that bit of rudeness and let Tom finish his meal,' Mrs D says.

I look down at my plate. It's still there. One lone meatball . . . with a very long black hair twisted through it. It looks like someone might have sewn the hair through the meat with a needle and thread. It is the thickest, blackest, greasiest hair in the world. It looks like it's from a horse's tail. Last I checked, the Danalises don't own a horse but, somehow, a horse has broken into Jack's kitchen while his mum was cooking and dipped its tail into the big pot of meatballs, leaving a special present for me before trotting off.

'Don't you like them?' Mrs D asks, looking hurt.

'I *love* them,' I say. And it's true. I do. There's a secret agreement between me and Mrs Danalis that we won't tell my mum that Mrs D's meatballs are my favourite food. 'I just had a big lunch. I'm full.' Saying this and knowing that it will mean no tiramisu makes me want to cry.

'Too full to finish my meatballs?' she says, horrified.

I stare into her eyes, then down at the meatball. I'd like to gently slide the hair out and flick it onto the floor, but they're watching me. Why did I have to get the hair? A family member could just be honest about this, but I'm a guest. I can't do that. If I embarrass Mrs D by telling her that there's part of a horse in my meatball, she may never let me stay here or cook me meatballs again.

'Bor-ing!' Barney chants, then he flings his plastic spoon at me. It glances off my face, smearing tomato sauce across my cheek before smacking the wall behind me.

Mr D's eyes flash and he leaps from his chair.

This could be my chance to rip the hair out.

'Just ignore it, please,' Mrs D warns.

Mr D sits.

Nuts. I was too slow.

Jack narrows his eyes and motions to the meatball, as if to say, *Just eat it!*

I take one last look around at the family. There's no way out of this. I have to take the plunge.

'I'm kidding,' I say. Mrs D looks up. 'Of course I'm not too full to eat my last meatball.'

She looks pleased.

I prod it with my fork. Juice flows from the puncture holes, runs down the length of the hair and pools on my plate. I raise it towards my face. They watch on. I move in slo-mo, giving ample time for someone to notice the hair and save me. But they don't. Are these people blind? How can five people around one table have their eyes on a single meatball and I'm the only one who can see the hair?

It reaches my lips, still warm, and I try to push it to the back of my mouth so that the whole thing goes in. I don't want to have to slurp the hair up like a spaghetti noodle. Then I swallow the meatball whole. It slides down my throat in one great lump, like I'm a python devouring a rat.

'Good boy,' Mrs D says, clapping her hands lightly. 'Jack, help me with the dishes, will

you?' She shoots Mr D a look. 'You too.' He starts clearing plates.

Jack and his folks take the dishes to the kitchen, leaving me and Barney at the table. Barney sticks his finger in his ear, scoops something brown and flaky out and eats it. This makes me slightly ill. I can still feel the giant lump in my throat. I take a sip of water but it's still there. I reach my thumb and forefinger into my mouth and feel around.

The hair seems to be wedged between my two bottom back teeth on the right-hand side. I pluck at it – *twang, twang* – trying to unhitch the hair. It won't budge. I get my fingers around the hair and pull hard. I realise that the meatball is still connected to the hair. It's hanging halfway down my throat, like meatball bungee.

'What you doing, boobyman?' Barney asks, but I barely hear him. I'm more focused on the giant lump of cow meat and horse hair stuck in my throat. My forehead erupts in sweat. Panic reaches up from my chest and clutches my throat.

I coil the hair around my finger, careful not to let it slip. I test the tension. I take a deep breath. Then I rip it towards the front of my mouth. The meatball launches up and out of my throat. It goes sailing between my lips and through the air. Tomato sauce spatters the tablecloth as it shoots across the table.

It seems to be heading right for Barney's face. I'd give my entire Batman comic collection to see it hit him but, if it does, I know he's going to squeal like a wounded pig and land me in a whole heap of trouble. I want to freeze time, snatch the meatball out of the air, feed it to the dog under the table and then press play again. But, unfortunately, that's not one of my superpowers. All I can do is watch, silently, as the meatball continues on its doomed voyage across the table.

Barney watches too, mouth gaping open, as it flies towards him.

Schloop.

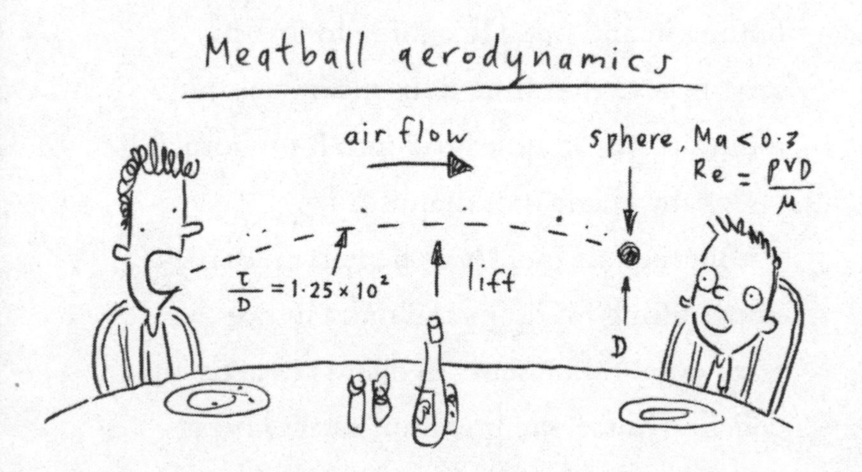

It lands right in his gob. It's unbelievable. I'm hopeless at basketball. I never hit free throws. And yet somehow I have managed to land a three-centimetre-wide meatball in a three-and-a-half-centimetre-wide hoop – Barney's pie hole.

There is a long pause as we both register the shock. You know how little kids leave a few seconds between when something bad happens and when they start to bawl their heads off? I think that's what's happening now.

I wait. His bottom lip quivers, then it starts huffing in and out. He's going to lose it. I can't believe this. If he dobs me in, tells his mum that I spat a meatball into his mouth, it'll wreck my chances of tiramisu.

But then, as quickly as he started, Barney stops huffing his lip in and out. His eyes glaze over and he starts to chew. He tastes the delicious sauce, the premium-quality meat, the sweet-smelling herbs and spices. He chews and chews . . . and he swallows the meatball, burying the evidence.

'Here we go!' Mrs D sings, entering the room with the chocolatey dessert of my dreams.

'Yummy in Barney tummy.'

'Yes, Barney loves tiramisu, don't you?' his mum says.

'No, Barney get extra *meatball*!'

I want to tell him to shut up.

Mr D and Jack come in carrying spoons and bowls.

'Big boy give me his last one,' Barney says, pointing at me.

I shake my head, trying to warn the little brat to be quiet.

'Big boy has a name, Barney. It's Tom. And big boy ate his own meatball.' She shakes her head and clicks her tongue, smiling at me. 'I don't know where he gets these ideas.'

'Kids,' I say, rolling my eyes. 'Could I please

use the bathroom?'

'Uh-uh,' Barney says. 'Big boy go PYOW! Meatball flyyyyy across table into Barney mouf.'

Mr D, Mrs D, Jack and I are all staring at Barney now.

'Barney, you know we don't like *lies*,' says Mr D. 'Even little ones.'

I worry when I hear the way Mr D says the word 'lies'. He suffers from CDS – Cranky Dad Syndrome – a terrible illness that many fathers come down with at some point in their lives. Once he gets started like this it can only lead to bad things.

'Barney NOT lie!' he screams at his dad.

'Don't you yell at me, young man,' says Mr D, his eye twitching slightly as the CDS takes hold.

'Daddy NO call Barney LIAR!'

'Okay, mister, off to bed.'

Uh-oh.

'NOOOOOOOOOOOOOOOOOOO!' Barney screams. 'Barney NO. GO. BED!'

'Say nigh-nigh,' says Mr D.

'Just wait,' Mrs D demands, holding up her hand.

Mr D doesn't listen. He's had enough. He picks Barney up off his chair. The little gremlin kicks and screams, throws the rest of his plastic cutlery and makes his body go stiff as a board. He's almost impossible to carry.

'Barney's a naughty boy!' says Mr D. 'Throwing his things around.'

'BARNEY NO NAUGHTY!!!'

'Yes, Barney tell fibs.'

'BARNEY. NO. TELL. PIGS!'

'Say nigh-nigh.'

'Barney no say nigh-nigh. Barney want timbuctoo.'

'No dessert for you.' Mr D carries him around the table towards me.

Mrs D yells, 'Stop!'

I've never seen a family meltdown like this. I feel terrible.

'Do you mind if I use the bathroom?' I ask again, nervous.

'Before you do, Tom,' Mrs D says. 'I'm sorry to ask but . . .'

Jack puts his head in his hands. 'Mum . . .'

'We have a bit of an issue at the moment with Barney and truth-telling,' she says. 'But I don't like seeing him upset like this. So, I have to ask the question . . .'

No. Please don't ask the question, I think.

'Is there any truth to what Barney's saying?

You didn't, somehow, give him your last meatball . . . did you?'

I stare at her. My mouth dries up. I look around at the family. I can either 'fess up and tell the truth, or let an innocent man take the rap for a crime he didn't commit. I want to say, *I'm sorry. He's telling the truth. I hauled the meatball up out of my throat by a horse hair that somehow made its way into your dinner, shot it into Barney's mouth and he ate it.*

But, just at that moment, Barney slaps me hard across the face with his tomato-saucey little hand. I wipe the sauce off, look him square in the eye, and say, 'No, Mrs D. Big boy not a liar. Barney telling fibs. Nigh-nigh, Barney.'

I give him a little wave and Mr D hauls him out of the room. Barney screams, 'BIG BOY DIIIIIIIE!'

His voice fades as he is dragged off down the hall.

'I'm very sorry about that, Tom,' says Mrs D. 'Tiramisu?'

'Yes, please,' I tell her.

She gives me an extra-large serve, and I think to myself, *Nigh-nigh, Barney. Nigh-nigh.*

As I go to dig into the tiramisu with my spoon, I notice something buried in the cream. I touch it with the tip of my spoon, and I realise that it has wings.

It is the biggest, blackest blowfly I have ever seen.

'Go on,' Mrs D says. 'Don't be polite.'

RecordBreakers

Me and Jack are pretty good at breaking stuff, so we've decided we're going to break a Guinness World Record. People set records all the time for the kind of dumb stuff that Jack and I do just for fun. So here's what we're going to attempt . . .

- **World's longest ear hair** – currently held by Anthony Victor of Madurai, India, who has ear hair 18.1 centimetres long (more than half a school ruler). I'm pretty sure my pop beat this when he was alive. I learned how to abseil on the hair from his right ear. And don't even get me started on his nose.

- **World's longest burp** – currently 1 minute, 13 seconds and 57 milliseconds by Michele Forgione of Italy. It is my life's dream to meet Michele Forgione and learn this ancient art form. My personal best is 5.7 seconds, thanks to Nan's broccoli and cheese muffins.

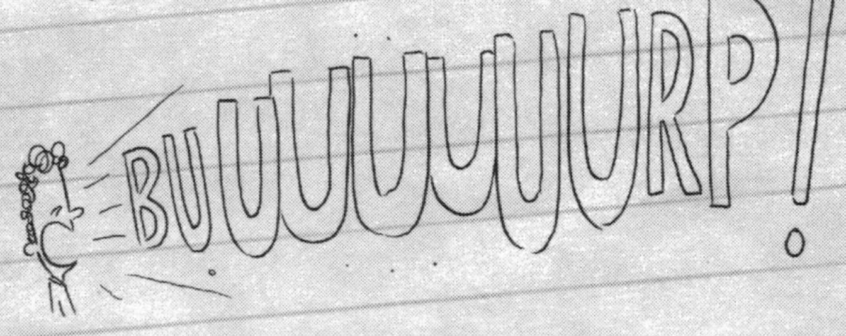

- **Heaviest weight lifted by nipples** – currently 32.6 kilograms (the average weight of an adult goat), held by 'The Baron' from Finland. I'm keen to attempt this. I just need to find the right goat.
- **Longest distance travelled keeping a table lifted with one's teeth** – currently 11.8 metres with a 12-kilogram table and a 50-kilogram person sitting on it. I once bit off

my sister Tanya's big toe when she wanted me to eat Vegemite off it. It was unbelievably chewy, so I figure my superhuman jaw strength should help me smash this one.

- **Fastest time to eat three extremely hot bhut jolokia chilli peppers** – currently 16.15 seconds by American Jason McNabb. I'll leave this one to Jack and tell him they're just cute little baby capsicums.

I'm also thinking of going for the blindfolded maggot-eating record by telling Jack they're rice bubbles.

Dance of the chilli peppers

- **Most spiders on the body for 30 seconds** – currently 200, achieved by Daniel Jovanovski of Macedonia. There are about 1000 huntsman spiders in our shed. I might start collecting them and remind Jack how Spider-Man got his powers.
- **Most clothes pegs clipped to the face in one minute** – currently 51 pegs by Italian Silvio Sabba. I once clipped 12 paperclips to my tongue. The guy in Emergency thought it was incredible. Mum, not so much.
- **Tallest toilet paper tower in 30 seconds** – currently 28 rolls, also achieved by Silvio Sabba in 2013. From an engineering point of view, I'm thinking three-ply toilet paper – the expensive stuff – might provide the greatest stability. And Jack is a Jenga master.

- **Most ice-cream scoops thrown and caught (in a cone) by a team of two in one minute** – currently 25 by Gabriele and Lorenzo Soravia of Germany. We figure this should be so easy that we don't even need to use cones. We're going to catch the scoops in our mouths – and eat them – within the minute. I'm thinking we'll beat the World Record for longest brain freeze at the same time.

- **World's longest fart.** I can't get an exact figure on the World Record, but I'm pretty sure it was Jack Danalis of Kings Bay, Australia, in my top bunk two nights ago during a sleep-over. No Guinness World Records officials were present, and Jack was asleep at the time, so it may not count, but he's confident he can do it again. We've put him on a strict diet of prunes and lentils.

If you could break any world record, what would it be? Let me know at TheTomWeekly@gmail.com

Runaway Car (Part One)

I hear the loud, non-stop honking of an old-fashioned car horn out front, and my heart sinks. It sounds like a flock of wounded geese. I should ignore it. I *need* to ignore it. But I don't. I go to the door and open it a crack. The heat of the day smacks me in the face and boils my eyeball juice. It's 40 degrees, the hottest day of summer so far. Nan is sitting in the driver's seat of a long, wide, shiny, light-blue 1952 Ford Crestline. A classic.

She honks the horn again and shouts, 'Come on, Tommy! Let's go for a drive.'

I open the door a little more and call out,

'It's too hot, Nan. I can't. Why don't you come inside and rest your weary bunions?'

She honks again. If Pop were alive he'd be furious that Nan was driving his pride and joy. Pop always kept the car garaged, shining it and tinkering with the engine, but he never drove it on the road. Now that he's gone, Nan likes to take it for a spin every now and then.

I wish Mum was home. She had to work today. There's no way she'd let me go with Nan. My grandmother is Australia's worst driver. Her top speed is 15 kilometres an hour. She drives so slowly that she makes time go backwards. She's a danger to herself and others.

Nan driving (this is NOT a driverless car).

Last time I rode with her she mowed down a stop sign, sideswiped a parked police car and smashed into the birdbath in the front yard of Mr Li's house at number 33.

She waves me over towards the car. I shouldn't go, but I feel sorry for her – so skinny and frail in that gigantic vehicle. I take a deep breath, hurry down the front steps and along the path. She has the Crestline sitting half on the kerb, half on the street.

'Hello, Tommy, love. Give your ol' Nan a kiss.' I lean through the passenger window. She looks like a little kid at the wheel. She has to sit on three fat phone books from 1984 just to see over the dashboard. Nan climbs off the books and shuffles across the seat so I can kiss her on the cheek. Her skin is soft and wrinkled and sweaty. The car's engine rumbles and grumbles and burbles. Steam hisses from the cracks around the edge of the bonnet. Pop must be spinning in his grave.

'You really shouldn't be driving, Nan,' I tell her.

'Why not?'

'You don't have a licence.'

'When I was a girl, you didn't need a licence. I've been driving since I was seven years old.'

'I didn't know cars were invented then.'

'Don't be a smartypants,' she says. 'Back in my day, I could reverse a tractor through a flock of sheep blindfolded. Don't you trust me?'

No is the answer, but she gets really mad when I question her driving skills.

'Yes, Nan, I trust you. It's just that . . . I've got homework. I –'

'Rubbish. You've never done homework in your life. Now get in. I'll buy you an iceblock and take you to the swimming pool.'

Sweat runs in ticklish rivers down the sides of my face. The sun grills the skin on my forehead like cheese on toast. I think about her offer. I weigh up the fear and embarrassment of being in the car with her against the sweet relief of the pool and the iceblock.

I open the passenger door and slide in.

'That's my boy,' she says, grinning and revving the engine twice.

I reach for my seatbelt and try to find the socket to slot it into, but it's not there.

'Must have fallen down the crack between the seats, love. Not to worry. Off we go.'

She jerks forward and I'm thrown back against the seat. I plunge my arm down into the seat crack. I find an old Mintie with sand all over it and a 'One Penny' coin before I find the socket for the belt. I pull it up, slot it in and tighten it until my guts are about to squeeze out of my ears.

'You have nothing to worry about,' she says.

She stomps on the accelerator, the tyres squeal, and we shoot out from the kerb. A car going by honks its horn and swerves, narrowly missing us.

Nan honks back. 'Nincompoop!' she screams. 'Sorry about that, Tommy. There are some crazy drivers on these roads.'

I pull my belt tighter and the car settles into Nan's 15-kilometre-an-hour crawl up the hill.

'Nan, the pool's at the other end of the street.'

‘I thought I’d get your iceblock from Papa Bear’s. You can eat it on the way. How does that sound?’

‘Thanks, Nan,’ I say as we continue to climb. Papa Bear’s is the shop up the hill on the corner of our street. My legs are sticking to the old vinyl seats in the heat, but it’s quite nice going this speed. You notice stuff you wouldn’t normally. Like that cat that just overtook us.

Oh no. My stomach sinks.

Brent Bunder and Jonah Flem are waiting to cross the street with their bikes about 40 metres up the hill. I slump down in my seat so I can’t be seen.

‘What’re you doing?’ Nan asks.

‘It’s comfy like this,’ I tell her. ‘Cooler.’ I look up and notice that the clouds are moving faster than we are.

‘Can you go any slower, Grandma?’ Jonah calls out as we drive by.

'Shut your gob, pipsqueak!' Nan screams. 'Respect your elders.'

Brent and Jonah laugh.

'Hey, is that you, Weekly?' Brent asks.

I slide down further into the seat.

'Hey, Weekly!' he calls.

The two boys pedal slowly alongside the car, looking down at me.

'Nice Sunday drive, mate?' Jonah asks. 'Why don't you just walk? It'd be faster.'

Nan swerves to the right and bumps one of their bikes. I sit up and look back to see Jonah checking his front wheel. 'Hey!' he shouts. 'You're a danger to society, lady!'

'Your face is a danger to mirrors!' Nan shouts back, peering through the steering wheel as we crawl up the hill. 'That showed them.'

'Nan, you're not really supposed to knock kids' bikes.'

'They're not kids. They're cane toads.

There's no law against squishing a couple of cane toads, is there?'

Just me and Nan on a leisurely Sunday drive.

I shrug. Flem and Bunder *are* kind of cane toad-ish. But the police might not see it that way if they report her. A few minutes later we roll up outside Papa Bear's. Nan slams into the rear bumper of the car parked out front, then rolls back downhill a few centimetres.

'There we go,' she says. 'What do you want, love? A Bubble O' Bill?'

Nan knows that I love Bubble O' Bills more than life itself. Especially on a flesh-meltingly hot day like today. I nod and grin.

'Two Bubble O' Bills coming right up.' She grabs her purse, climbs down off the phone books, exits the car and slams the door. She slams it so hard that the car wobbles from side to side. There's a screeking sound of metal on metal, the suspension groans, and the car starts to roll slowly backwards.

'Nan!' I shout, but she's shuffling along in front of the car now and doesn't hear me.

I look to the dashboard and see a handle that says 'Park Brake' in faded white lettering. I reach across and yank it hard. The handle heaves back towards me . . . and snaps off in my hand. I scream and throw the handle into the back seat.

'Nan!'

She disappears inside the shop and I'm picking up speed. I've rolled about five metres down the hill and I'm heading towards a silver hatchback parked on the kerb. I could open the door and jump out, but I'd hit the gutter pretty hard.

I peel my sweaty legs off the seat and slide across until my hip hits the pile of phone books. I jerk the wheel to the right in a desperate attempt to miss the parked car. The back of Nan's car veers out into the road and another car swerves around me, the driver slamming his fist on the horn. I'm heading diagonally across the street now, so I pull the wheel back towards me to stay on the left side of the road.

I'm really moving now. I chuck the phone books onto the passenger floor and slide behind the wheel. I'm looking back over my shoulder and trying to steer, but I haven't driven a car recently – or ever – so it's a bit difficult. My feet are tap dancing, trying to find the brake pedal. It must be down there somewhere.

Jonah and Brent are in the middle of the road.

'Get out of the way!' I shout out the window. I look for the horn and slam my fist down on the big 'Ford' logo in the middle of the steering wheel.

Waaaaaaaarp! The horn blurts.

I look back through the rear windscreen. Brent and Jonah look up at the car speeding towards them. We all scream.

To be continued on page 180

So, this is the future.
It will be when we get a licence to drive it.

Shirt

'Mum, where's my school shirt?' I yell from my room.

'The same place it is every day,' she calls from the bathroom.

'Where's that?'

'In your drawer.'

'It's not there.'

'Have you looked?'

'Yep.'

Mum growls, but it doesn't worry me. We do this every day. My school shirts always go missing. I think she kind of enjoys it. Like a game of hide-'n'-seek. Adults don't get to have fun very often.

'Well, have another look!' she shouts. 'I find opening my eyes works quite well.'

'My eyes are open.'

'Will you two be quiet?!' my sister, Tanya, screams from her room. 'I've still got five minutes till I have to get up. I need my beauty sleep.'

'You're gonna need a lot longer than five minutes,' I tell her.

'Shut up, Tom.'

'If I come in there, I'm just going to find it immediately. Then I'll be annoyed for the rest of the day,' Mum says. 'So have another look, Tom.'

'It's not here!' I insist.

Another growl.

Footsteps.

Mum walks into my room.

I'm lying on the bed in my pyjamas

reading a Tintin book called *The Broken Ear.*

She stops in the doorway. 'What are you doing?'

'Reading a Tintin book called *The Broken Ear.*'

'Why are you reading?'

'I thought you liked it when I read?'

Mum rubs her forehead with the palm of her hand and sighs loudly. This is never a good sign. 'I do, but you're supposed to be looking for your shirt.'

'I can't find it.'

She walks over and opens my top-right drawer. 'Look what I found!' she says, holding up a school shirt.

'Oh, thanks.'

She stands there staring at me. I appreciate her finding the shirt, but I'd kind of like to be left in peace now.

'Did you even *look* in this drawer?' she asks.

'Nope.'

'Why not? It's clearly labelled with the words "school shirts". See? Right here.' She points at the label a little too aggressively.

'Oh, yeah,' I say.

'This is where your school shirts go.'

'I forgot.'

'Aaaaaaaaaaaargh!' she screams.

I sit up. Screaming is Mum's little way of telling me that she's feeling a wee bit frustrated.

'You'll *actually* be the death of me, Tom Weekly.'

'Geez, it's just a shirt.'

'Put. It. On,' she hisses and slouches out of the room.

Sometimes she gets like this in the morning – touchy for no reason at all.

I put my shirt on and look in my drawer, scratching my bum.

'Mum!' I call out.

'Yes?' she shouts back, her voice trembling.

'Do you know where my shorts are?'

Writer's Block

I have something to admit. I've been suffering from writer's block. That's where you can't think of anything to write, so you just sit there staring at the page like a numpty. I didn't think writer's block was a real thing until recently. I thought it was something writers made up so they didn't have to work, which is pretty genius of them, really. I wish teachers would invent 'teacher's block', where they couldn't think of anything to teach so they'd just sit there, drooling and staring at the whiteboard six hours a day. And I wish Mr Skroop, the Deputy Principal, would come down with

‘Skrooper’s block’, so he wouldn’t be so . . . Skroopy all the time.

But writer’s block is no joke – my brain is officially dead. Zombies wouldn’t bother eating it. Even for an entree. The worst part is that I know why I have it, and I know how to cure it. But the solution could mean the end of my writing career.

It's Sunday morning and I have been lying on my bed, staring at a blank notebook for hours. Yesterday . . . the same thing. I can't go on like this. I owe it to the world to continue to share my gift for telling stories about scabs and missing body parts and sloppy food and head lice.

I lean over to the bookshelf next to my bed. I reach behind the first row of books and feel around until my hand rests on *Natrix's Big Book of Magic.* It is a hefty tome with a carved wooden cover, about ten centimetres thick. I lift it out and look at it for a few seconds, my heart hammering away. I open it. Inside, there is a rectangular hole carved within the pages, and inside that is a little green box. I take out the box and rest it in the palm of my hand.

Don't do it, some part of me whispers. *This is wrong.*

I lift the lid of the box, revealing tiny crystals and shells and the tip of a magpie

feather. I remove the false bottom of the box, and underneath lies the answer to my problems. It seems to pulse with a green, magical glow. My fingers are magnetically drawn to it. I reach in and take out a single, gnarled toenail. My very last one. I hold it up to the light from my reading lamp above my bed, and I actually salivate.

I have never admitted this to anyone but . . . all of my stories have been written while chewing on my grandfather's toenails.

There. I've said it.

People always ask me where I get my insane story ideas. Well, now you know. I'm not proud of it. I mean, it's one thing to chew on your pop's toenies when he's alive. Quite another thing to do it after he's, you know . . . not.

I first got a taste for toenies when I was two years old. My fangs were coming through and I'd lost my teething toy, so I started jawing on Pop's toenails to ease the pain in my mouth. Mum tried to stop me but Pop thought it was hilarious, a story he could tell his mates.

'Leave the boy alone,' he'd say. 'He can't help being part dog.'

Pop would tell me stories while I chewed on his toenies. And even when my teeth came through I didn't stop. I used to bite those knobbly yellow husks right off his foot. I loved listening to Pop's tales about epic thumb-wrestling contests in the trenches during the war and billycart crashes and heroic efforts on the cricket pitch when he was a kid.

It kept going till I was about five, when Mum told me I wasn't allowed to do it anymore. She said it was unhygienic and weird.

But it was too late. I was hooked. Pop never wore shoes, so I could always tell when he had a ripe nail on the go. I couldn't wait to snip it. It must have been my ancient hunter-gatherer instincts kicking in. I started chopping Pop's nails with regular clippers for a while, but the nails were too tough. I went through seven sets of clippers in two years.

So I put together a little kit – tin snips, a hacksaw, a rusty metal file and a small set of chisels. I would visit Pop every few weeks, and he'd tell me stories while I worked. When I was finished, I'd put the toenies into a plastic sandwich bag and take them home to snack on.

Then, the Christmas I turned nine, I read Paul Jennings' book *Unreal* and decided to start writing my own stories. On Boxing Day morning I sat at the dining table with a Santa hat on, ready to write, but my mind was blank. Without thinking, I cracked open my bag of toenies – a toenie always makes a man feel better – and my pen started moving. It felt like I was possessed with the power of all the tall tales that Pop had told me over the years while I'd been gnawing on his feet. I wrote and wrote all day long and into the night.

Then, a little over six months ago, as I

sat on Pop's rickety footstool in the nursing home, I sawed off his last toenie. I didn't know at the time that it would be the last one. Pop prattled away about his battles with the other nursing home inmates, the disgusting meatballs he was served for lunch and his latest plan for escape. With one final stroke of my little hacksaw, the nail fell from Pop's foot and skittered across the linoleum floor. It was magnificent – one of the biggest toenies I had ever seen – so I picked it up and dropped it into the sandwich bag with the other nine delicious nails. I quickly said goodbye, disappeared into the hallway and rushed out the front door of the nursing home.

As soon as I was back in my bedroom, notebook ready, pen in hand, my greedy fingers delved into the bag, chose a medium-sized toenie and jammed it into the corner of my mouth. I began to chew and the words started to flow.

I know it's sick, but I can't help it. When you get a taste for toenies at an early age, it's very difficult to give up. I feel most alive when I'm nibbling on one. Pop's toenails had played football for the 1959 New South Wales under-17s rugby squad. They had carried him down the aisle when he got hitched to Nan. They had fought for their country in Vietnam. They told better stories than any book.

They're dangerous, too. If you aren't careful and you swallow one whole, it can slit you right open. I once devoured a toenie and it scratched me all the way down through my throat, stomach and intestines for two days. I was worried it'd get stuck inside . . . but it came out alright. The pain was mind-boggling.

If only I'd known that we wouldn't have Pop with us much longer, I wouldn't have let my supplies run down. He died so suddenly six months ago, in the lead-up to Fast Eddie's Hot Dog Eat. I only had 20 toenails in storage and I've been writing so much I've eaten 19 of them.

I know exactly what you're thinking. I've already considered farming other old people's toenails. Nan's aren't bad but they're too small and dainty, and they take forever to grow. They don't snap between your teeth, and she bathes so regularly that they have no smell. The flavour is disappointing, too, like a pretzel without salt or a cupcake without icing. They're just too . . . nice. Edible but forgettable.

So, here I am, staring at the last toenie glistening in the light of the reading lamp. It is shaped like a crescent moon and coated in a thin film of soil or yeasty toe jam, I'm not sure which. It seems to stare back at me, like it can see right into my soul. I already know what it will taste like – sweet and savoury, like a block of Vegemite chocolate. I could get two or three days out of it if I'm careful. But it's the last thing I have to remember Pop by. Do I really want to devour the last trace of my grandfather?

I look down at the blank page of my notebook. If I do eat it, what extraordinary story will I tell with that toenie between my teeth? Will I get a whole book out of it? And will it be the last book I ever write? What if, once the toenies are gone, that's it – my creative tank is dry forever?

The thought scares me, but I know I have to be brave. That's what Pop would have wanted. I raise it to my mouth. I feel it between my teeth. I feel the magic and wonder of Pop's stories wash over me.

I pick up my pen and, just like that, I begin to write. Slowly at first, but then a story starts to trickle in, something about a muffin attack.

I dedicate the following story to the one and only Cliff Weekly – hot-dog eating champion, world's angriest grandpa, nursing home escape artist and grower of the gnarliest, most delicious toenails in the southern hemisphere.

Pop, you're a legend.

When you're done reading this book, maybe you could write a story of your own. I'm not telling you to eat anyone's toenails. That would be sick and wrong, and it's probably done all sorts of harm to my guts, but you can find your own story inspiration. For you, it might be eating the sleep from your dog's eye. Or the wax from your cat's ear. Or, I know this sounds weird, but you could even try not eating human or animal bits at all. Gnaw on the end of a lucky pen, perhaps? Whatever you do, good luck. May the toenies be with you.

(Seriously, don't eat dog sleep or cat wax. You may start barking or meowing.)

Reverse Halloween

We're doing 'Reverse Halloween' again this year. It's a tradition where Mum spends the day baking muffins and cookies, then we go around and give them to the neighbours rather than asking for lollies. No tricks. No treats.

Mum says, 'Kindness and compassion for others are the most important qualities in a human being.' But I say, 'Lollies are the most important nutrient in the food pyramid.' It's only a matter of time before the scientists work it out.

Knock-knock-knock.

Unlikely Moments in Science #12

We wait. I grind my teeth.

'Stop scrinching your teeth,' Mum snips.

The door swings open and Harriet, the old lady from number 42, answers. 'Hell-ooo!'

'Happy Reverse Halloween!' Mum shouts. 'Can I interest you in a muffin or a cookie?'

'Well, what a surprise! Don't mind if

I do,' Harriet says, wiping her hands on a paint-spattered apron. She's new to the neighbourhood and seems to spend most of her time painting the dozens of creepy ceramic gnomes dotted around her garden.

Harriet pushes open the security door as Mum peels back the red-and-white polka dot tea towel covering her basket. The muffins look soft and golden, pocked with white chocolate chunks and plump red berries. The cookies are so chocolatey that even my nostrils are salivating. My mother is not widely known for being a brilliant chef, but these are the best looking things she's ever made. I'm allowed to have one of each when we get home if I'm not too 'grinchy' while we're Reverse Halloween-ing.

'They're sugar-free, dairy-free, gluten-free and vegan.'

I hang my head. Why does she have to ruin everything? I specifically told her not to mention this to anyone. She might as well just say right up front, 'They taste like pencil shavings! Run for your life!'

'Oh, how lovely,' Harriet croons. She chooses a muffin and says, 'I think I might have some sweets in here for this young man.'

'Thanks!' I say quickly.

'No thanks!' Mum cuts in. 'We like to *give* on Halloween rather than receive – don't we, Tom?'

That's Christmas! my mind screams. Although, deep down, I probably prefer to receive at Christmas, too. (That's strictly off the record.)

'Tom?' Mum says again.

'Yes, Mum. We like to give,' I say through gritted teeth.

'Oh,' Harriet says. 'Well . . . can I at least give you a piece of fruit, love?'

I glunch at Mum through my eyebrows. ('Glunch' is an old Scottish word that Nan uses, which means 'an angry glare'. I kind of like it. *Glunch*.)

'That would be lovely, Harriet. Say thank you, Tom.'

'Thank you, Tom,' I say glunchily.

She toddles off into the house.

'Worst. Halloween. Ever,' I whisper to Mum.

Harriet returns moments later holding an orange.

An *orange*.

She hands it to me.

'Ooo, what a lovely orange,' Mum says.

It's slightly mouldy on one side, and the skin is thin and brownish. A couple of fruit flies orbit around its cratered surface.

'Grown from my own tree. Make sure you share it with your mum,' Harriet says. 'Happy Halloween!' She pulls her screen door closed and waves us off with a smile.

We walk up the path past all the demonic garden gnomes, who laugh and snicker about my festy orange. A bunch of high-school kids run past us towards Harriet's front door, wielding plastic knives and chainsaws. They are dressed as ghosts and ninja pumpkins and zombie dogs.

Out on the footpath, a stream of kids walk up and down the street, smiling through the fake blood dripping out of their faces, carrying bags full of delicious, sugary morsels filled with genetically modified high-fructose corn syrup and luscious preservatives.

I can't take it anymore. I drop the stinking orange into Mum's basket and turn for home. 'I'm not doing this.'

'Why not?' she asks. 'When you're an adult you'll realise –'

'Yeah, but I'm not an adult!' I interrupt. 'I'm a kid. Of course you love mouldy oranges. You're, like, 80 years old.'

'Forty,' she corrects.

I keep walking.

Mum follows. 'Suit yourself. No muffin or cookie for you.'

I keep walking, but I know I have no choice but to turn around. Even if they are everything-free, Mum may never cook something that looks this good again. I stop. I turn. I can't believe what I see. Mum is standing at our next-door neighbour's gate, opening the latch. The gate has a small gold sign with black lettering that reads, 'No Visitors, Please'. It's the neighbour who I told her we will not be giving a muffin to *under any circumstances*.

'No. Way,' I warn. 'We are *not* giving Mr Skroop a muffin!' I whisper fiercely. Deputy Principal Skroop is not my biggest fan. By which I mean he would like to have my heart in a jar on his desk. Mister Fatterkins, Skroop's enormous orange cat, sits in the front window, hissing at me. The cat's saliva runs down the window pane.

'This is an opportunity for us to build a bridge with Mr Skroop, to repair your relationship.'

Mum's been reading books by the Dalai Lama again. She says her religion is 'kindness'. But my religion is lollies.

She walks up the white painted path towards his house. The grass in the front yard is like a golf course putting green, dotted with thorny pink and white rosebushes.

'Mum! *No!*' I whisper.

I should be running away, but she must be stopped. You're not supposed to feed wild animals. She's gone mad. Maybe she overheated her brain in the kitchen when she was baking the muffins. I told her to turn the exhaust fan on. No one knocks on Skroop's door on Halloween . . . or any other night of the year. He's probably in there eating the last kid who did. I want to run for my life, but I need that muffin and cookie.

I run up the path and grab her arm as she's about to knock on the door. 'Mum, don't do it.'

'Let go, Tom,' she says.

'Please. He's crazy. He's a monster. He's –'

Suddenly I am staring up into the soulless, charcoal eyes of Mr Skroop. He opened the door just as I said the words, 'He's a monster.'

Skroop is a very tall, very skinny man. He is wearing his maroon cardigan, shredded at the shoulder from the razor-sharp claws of Mr Fatterkins, who is perched there on his shoulder now, like a second head. His face is so thin and pale, if I didn't know him I'd think he was wearing a *Scream* mask.

'*What do you want*?' he snaps.

Mum looks a bit frightened now.

'H-h-happy Reverse Halloween!' she says. 'We were wondering if you'd like a muffin? Or perhaps a cookie?'

She seems like a little girl, looking up into

the big black holes of Skroop's nostrils.

'I despise Halloween,' he says. 'American rrr-rubbish.' He rolls the 'r' for extra evilness.

'But this is *Reverse* Halloween,' Mum says. 'It's the opposite, where we give rather than receive.'

'Isn't that Christmas?' Skroop asks.

For a moment, Skroop and I speak the same language.

He looks from Mum to the basket, suspicious.

'Well, let me see them!' he says. 'I don't have all day. It's almost Mr Fatterkins' dinnertime.'

Mum pulls back the polka dot tea towel and looks up again, hopeful, like she really cares what Skroop thinks of her cooking.

He scowls. Mr Fatterkins glares at the basket like he's ready to pounce.

'The muffins are wh-white chocolate and raspberry,' she says. 'And the cookies are chocolate chip. With extra chips.'

He looks from the basket to me. 'You didn't have anything to do with the baking process, did you, Weekly?'

'No, Mr Skroop.'

He reaches down towards the basket. He selects a cookie. It's the one that I'd had my eye on, the filthy scoundrel. The chocolate-chippiest one. He turns it upside down and inspects it, then looks at the top again. He runs his index finger along the surface, sniffs it, then his pointy little tongue shoots out and he licks the cookie. It's one of the most disgusting things I've ever seen.

He looks at Mum, then at me, disgusted. He raises the cookie and pops it into the mouth of Mr Fatterkins, who devours it in two bites, like a dog would snaffle a biscuit.

Without another word, Skroop slams the door right in our faces.

Bang!

Mum looks at me, her mouth open in shock. 'I can't believe that,' she says.

'That's Skroop for you,' I say.

'He is the *rudest* man I have ever met.'

'Tell me about it,' I say. I'm glad that Mum has finally seen the light. I tug on her arm, hoping we can head back home now, maybe even cancel the Reverse Halloween tradition altogether.

But Mum won't budge. She clenches her fist and stares into her basket. 'I spent *hours* baking these things. I took the afternoon off work to walk around the neighbourhood and reach out to my fellow humans, and he has the hide to –'

'Mum, *shhhhh*. Let's just go.'

Then she does the unthinkable. She pounds on Skroop's door.

'No, Mum, don't. Please, I'm too young to die.'

'I'm going to give him a piece of my mind,' she says.

'Evil doesn't listen to reason. It's not worth it.' I try to pull her away from the door. 'Remember when he rubbed Lewis's head on mine and gave me nits? Remember when I kicked my football over the fence and he chopped it up and posted it into the letterbox? Remember when he ate my scab?'

She's not listening to anything I say. She's on the warpath. *Bang-bang-bang.* She peers through the window beside the door. 'I know you're in there, Walton!' she calls. 'How dare you feed my cooking to that hideous cat!'

'He loves the cat,' I say. 'Maybe it was a compliment. Remember what the Dalai Lama says: kindness and compassion for others are the most important qualities in a human being. Poor old Mr Skroop's probably just having a bad day.'

Her shoulders slump. I'm so relieved. I really need that muffin now to settle my nerves.

But then the door swings open again. Skroop and Fatterkins loom over us. There are cookie crumbs on Skroop's shoulder. I'm hoping Mum doesn't notice.

'Get off my property immediately or I shall call the police.'

And I know he will. He's called the cops on me before. He's so sensitive. I did accidentally burn down his fence that one time, but still . . .

'I want an apology,' Mum demands.

'Walton Skroop does not apologise, especially to the mother of one of the greatest nitwits ever to attend Kings Bay Public School.'

'Did you just call my son a *nitwit*?'

Uh-oh.

'*Did* you?' she demands.

Skroop retreats a step. 'As you refuse to remove yourself from my land, I have no other choice.' He picks up the receiver of an old-fashioned phone sitting on the hall stand and starts to dial. Mum goes to snatch it from him and Mr Fatterkins shoots out a long ginger paw, scratching her across the hand.

'OWWW!' Mum shrieks.

She's bleeding. It looks like a fake Halloween scar, only there's real blood dripping onto Skroop's stoop.

'Yes, hello, I'd like to report an intruder,' Skroop says.

'An intruder?' Mum squawks. She takes a single muffin and hurls it at him. It smacks him in the nose, leaving a red raspberry smudge, glances off and knocks the phone from his hand.

He's shocked. '*Hello? Hello?*' a small voice says from the phone receiver that's now doing the backspin in Skroop's front hallway.

'Mum, take it easy,' I say, but she grabs a cookie from the basket and hurls it at Fatterkins. The cat screeches and leaps from Skroop's shoulder before the choc-chip missile makes contact.

Mum reaches for another cookie and throws it like a ninja star at Skroop. The cookie hits him on the forehead. He squeals and clutches his brow.

'*Hello? Can you hear me?*' says the voice on the phone.

Skroop snatches it up, still holding his forehead. He slams the door shut with a bang and yells into the phone, 'Yes. I have just been attacked by a woman with a basket of baked goods. Biscuits and cakes and the like. It was terrifying. They were slightly burnt, possibly gluten-free and very, very hard. I think I have a concussion.'

'They were *not* hard!' Mum shouts and throws another muffin at the door. *Thunk*. It leaves a large dent. 'Oh . . . Okay, they were slightly firm!'

'Mum, it's time to go,' I say. I take her by the arm and lead her down the stairs, along the white painted path and out of the disturbing land of Skrooptopia.

I sit her down at the dining table. She's shaking and muttering things to herself. I pry the basket from her hand and rest it on the kitchen bench. I flick on the jug to make a cup of tea and drag a chair across to the pantry. I reach into the top and pull down a packet of ginger nut biscuits – her favourite.

I make the tea and put it beside the biscuits.

'You really got worked up back there,' I say.

'I'm sorry.' She mops at her tears with a snotty, balled-up tissue.

'It's okay. You stood up to Skroop in a way I never would have. You're kind of my hero right now.'

She forces a smile.

I take a bite out of a cookie. It's sweet, moist and delicious, despite being sugar-free, dairy-free, gluten-free and vegan. It tastes even sweeter when I think of Skroop copping one in the face. Maybe I was wrong about Reverse Halloween all along.

'Mum?'

'Yes,' she says, sipping her tea, her hand still shaking.

'Can we do Reverse Halloween again next year?

What Would You Rather Do?

Jack stayed over at my place last night. We had an epic round of 'What Would You Rather Do?' till about 9.00, when Mum said, 'Lights out. Night, boys.' We kept playing till 9.30, when she said, 'Time to go to sleep. See you in the morning.' So we whispered till 10.30, when Mum poked her head in on her way to bed and said, 'Are you still awake? Go to sleep *now*, Tom Weekly, or there'll be consequences. By the way, this room smells like farts. Good night.'

We couldn't help ourselves. It was so fun. We kept playing till 11.42, when Jack laughed raucously and Mum stormed in wearing her dressing-gown and a slathering of weird cream on her face, her hair all wild, screaming like the Abominable Snowman. It was one of the scariest things I've ever seen. Jack reckons it gave him nightmares and he's never sleeping over again. Anyway, here are some of the devilish dilemmas we devised.

Would you rather . . .

- Drink a tablespoon of bright yellow pus or eat 13 fresh scabs?
- Be buried alive in marshmallows or Smarties?
- Eat a whole jar of Vegemite or a stick of butter?
- Eat cheesy Vegemite sausages wrapped in marshmallow or peanut butter sausages wrapped in bacon?
- Find the tip of someone's finger in your cheeseburger or a rat's tail in your fries?

- Be turned into a frog for a year or a cane toad for a week?
- Get hit by lightning or never use technology again?
- Get a needle though the eye or have your bum set on fire?
- Ride rodeo-style on the back of a great white shark or an angry rhino?

- Wake up and you're the only person left on earth, or die and everyone else survives?
- Spend the night alone in a haunted house or run through a mall full of zombies?

- Travel into the future or into the past? (And you can't come back.)
- Get hit by a speeding bus or sat on by an elephant?
- Get trapped under ice or be buried alive?
- Tightrope walk over a swimming pool of vomit or bungee jump over a volcano?
- Put a thumbtack under your toenail and kick a concrete wall or have paper cuts all over your body and jump into a pool of lemon juice?

Tom Weekly: Child Genius

I. Am. A genius. An absolute genius. It's Friday morning, 10.12 am. I should be in school. But I'm not.

'Didn't the Friday morning maths test start 42 minutes ago?' you may ask.

And you would be correct. But I am unable to take part in this morning's maths test because I, Tom Weekly, am in my favourite place in the world: Nan's red velvet couch, feet up, with a colourful crocheted blanket over my legs and a nice, warm remote control in my hand.

As I flick through the channels I can smell

Nan's homemade sourdough bread in the toaster. I'm tossing up whether to do a Disney Channel comedy marathon or watch every *Iron Man* movie back-to-back. I can hear Nan out in the kitchen, whistling while she poaches two eggs for me, slightly runny with a single twist of salt from the grinder, just the way I like them.

Life doesn't get much better than this.

Meanwhile, Jack and Lewis and all the other suckers in my class are in the middle of another soul-crushing, hour-long Friday morning maths exam.

I turned in an Oscar-worthy performance this morning. Mum didn't even question whether I had a stomach-ache or not. Usually she knows I'm faking right away, but I swear my acting is getting better all the time. I should run workshops for other kids.

Nan is padding down the hall in her slippers. She appears at the lounge room

doorway, carrying a large tray. She's thin and small but very strong. She beats me every time we thumb wrestle.

'There you go, love,' she says, resting my tray on the coffee table. 'Sorry it took me so long. How are you feeling?'

'I'm okay, Nan,' I croak.

'Oh, you brave soldier.'

I've found over the years that it's much better to say that you're okay – just battling on, trying not to bother anyone – rather than complaining about how sick you are all the time.

There is a large glass of freshly squeezed orange juice beside my hot buttered toast and perfectly poached eggs. I have an appetite the size of a buffalo. I had to skip breakfast at home so that Mum would believe I was sick. Next time I might have to fake a cold so that it doesn't interfere with my meals.

'How's your temperature?' she asks, resting her hand on my forehead.

I give her my best puppy-dog eyes.

'Not too bad,' she says, 'but you take it easy. I don't like it when you're unwell. You watch your movie and eat up your breakfast. That'll make you big and strong.'

Fake sick days are made even better when Nan speaks to me like I'm four years old and uses words like 'big and strong' and 'brave soldier'. I also like it when she says 'tummy' and 'blankie'.

I sit up slowly and swing my legs off the couch with a groan, but not too loud.

'Thanks, Nan,' I say, my throat just a little husky.

I pick up my fork and run my knife across the egg. The yolk spills over Nan's famous sourdough. She's watching me so I chew slowly, carefully, as though I'm not really sure if I can keep it down. She eases herself into her rocking chair. My nan has an *actual* rocking chair. Like a grandmother in an apple pie ad.

After I eat my eggs and guzzle my juice a little too quickly, I pull my feet back onto the couch. Nan tucks me in with the dirty Humpty Dumpty stuffed toy I used to drag around when I was little. I'm just about to click *play* on the remote when there's a knock at the door.

'Good heavens,' Nan says.

'Who is it?' I ask, a single note of worry tapping the triangle in my heart.

'I don't know, love. I . . . What day is it?'

'Friday,' I say. It's 10.25 now, which makes me feel warm all over, knowing that Jack's brain is being squished to death by the world's heaviest maths test.

'Oh, I forgot about the girls,' Nan says. 'Look at the state of me. I haven't even got my gear on.'

'What girls?' I ask. 'What gear?'

'Hello-oo!' says a high-pitched voice from behind the front door.

'Coming!' Nan says, patting her hair down and straightening her bright green and orange striped dress.

'What girls?' I ask again, already knowing who the 'girl' at the front door is but praying for it not to be true.

She twists the deadlock and opens the door.

'Hello!' screams Sue Danalis – Jack's grandmother and Nan's new best friend. They used to be mortal enemies, but a couple of months ago they discovered yoga at the same time. Now they're joined at the artificial hip. Sue is very short, very wide (although not quite as wide as she used to be after two months of yoga) and very loud. She squeezes Nan into a bear hug and lifts her off her feet. Then she sees me. My face drops.

'Who's that on your couch?' Sue asks. 'Is that your *boyfriend*?'

'Certainly is,' Nan says.

Sue calling me Nan's boyfriend makes me feel a bit uneasy. Nan is 63 years older than me. And she's my grandmother.

'He was feeling crook. Had the day off school.'

'Ooooh, you weren't *faking*, were you?' Sue asks, pointing a long fingernail painted with hideous orange polish at me.

'No,' I gasp, but my eyes tell a different story, and Sue knows it.

She clicks her tongue and shakes her head. 'I had four boys of my own, and I know when a boy is telling porky-pies, believe you me.'

I smile in a sickly way and turn to the TV. I really don't like the way she saw right through me. Best not to look at her. I hit the *play* button on *Iron Man* and turn up the volume. The warning comes up: 'Do not copy movie or you'll be poached in molten lava.'

'Now, you give your Aunty Sue a kiss,' she says, heading across the lounge room towards me. She places what can only be a broccoli quiche on the coffee table. It may also have carrot in it. I can spot concealed vegetables from 20 paces.

'No,' I say. 'I can't. I'm sick. I don't want to make you –' But it's too late. She's leaning down towards me. I can see my reflection in her spectacles. I really do look sick now – and terrified.

'I know how much you love a kiss from your Aunty Sue,' she says.

(Can I just say, for the record, that that is *not* true.)

I try turning my head away but it's no good. Those big, red, lipsticky lips are like heat-seeking missiles locked on target. I swear she has more hair on the mole on her chin than I have on my head. I let out a little squeal as she plants a big fat kiss right on the corner of my mouth. It's terrible. It's ghastly. I have a flashback of Stella Holling kissing me in the playground. But I'd rather kiss Stella a thousand times than be kissed on the corner of the mouth by Sue again. Then I think of the Friday morning maths test, and I'd probably rather kiss Sue a thousand times than do that.

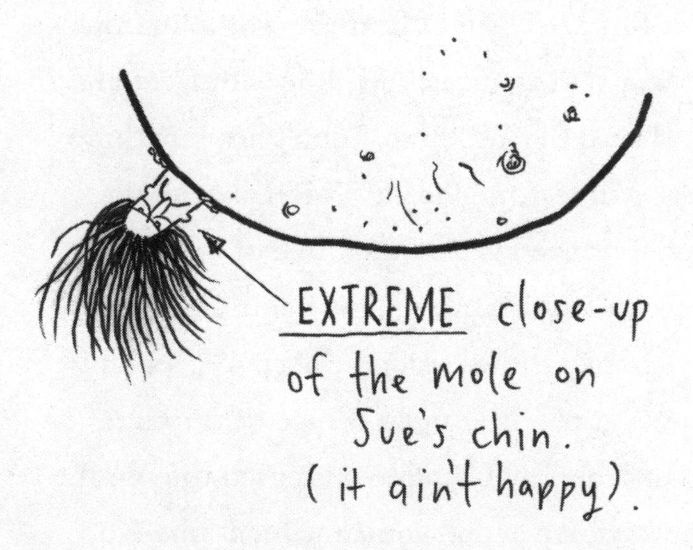

'Good morning!' another voice chirps. Sue stands and we both turn to the open front door, where three more elderly women are entering the house. That makes five ladies crowded into Nan's lounge room. They are all wearing colourful tracksuits and squawking in extremely loud voices over the top of one another, like a flock of rosellas – three conversations at once. I can't follow any of it, but I'm pretty sure I hear the words 'ingrown toenail', 'frozen wart' and 'bowel movements'.

I turn the TV up so I don't hear anything that will scar me for life. This makes all the ladies notice me, and the three of them who have just arrived shriek my name and shuffle over. They gather around the couch, looking down at me. It's Sandra Wingett from the cake shop, Fay Crabtree who used to own the newsagency, and a woman named Julie who lives at the nursing home. Julie has hair so white you could ski down it, and thick, black-rimmed glasses.

'Heavens above. Look at you, Thomas Weekly,' she says. 'You were knee-high to a grasshopper last time I saw you!'

'How's school going?' Sandra asks.

'What's your favourite subject?' Fay wades in.

'Do you like your teacher?' Julie says.

'How's your mum?'

'And that rascal Bando?'

'You're not still friends with that hooligan, Jack, are you?' Jack's nan asks.

They don't even wait for me to answer before the next question rolls in.

'Is your sister enjoying high school?'

'Do you have a girlfriend? I bet she's pretty.'

'What's her name?'

'You look just like my grandson, Rex. Is he in your class? He's in year two.'

I take this last one as a personal insult. I'm short, but I'm not *that* short.

'Do you feel okay?' Julie asks.

I want to say, *Not anymore.* And it's true. I actually do feel a bit queasy.

'Let's leave him to rest,' Sue says, pulling up my blanket. 'The poor boy is *soooo* sick.' She does a big fake wink and cackles.

'Leave him alone, Sue,' Nan says.

The other ladies place their casserole dishes and big pots of soup on the coffee table. The place now reeks – a sickening mix of cauliflower, broccoli, sweet potato, stinky cheese, lentils and perfume.

'Nancy, where's your VHS player?' Sandra asks, ferreting around in the cabinet under the TV.

NEWSFLASH!

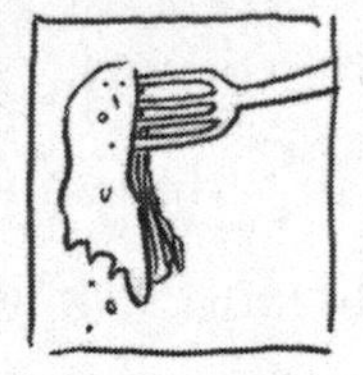

Scientists from Norway recently concluded in a 3 year study, the findings many had already suspected; that old people do indeed smell like wet spinach and mothballs. The reason is still unknown.

'I was watching something!' I say, but she doesn't seem to hear me.

'Just under the record player on top of the TV,' Nan calls back.

Fay pops the old videotape in and the opening credits of a show called *Yoga Oz-Style* start to play. The picture is scratchy and it jumps all over the place. The show looks like it was recorded in 1932.

'C'mon, girls, let's get this over with so we can have some food,' Sue says. 'I could eat the bum out of a low-flying duck.'

A couple of the women laugh, and they slip off their jackets and tracksuit pants. Underneath, they reveal tight-fitting exercise outfits. Sue's is hot-pink, Mrs Wingett's is a fluorescent yellow onesie, and Fay Crabtree is sporting blinding orange leg warmers with matching sweatbands.

'Sorry, Tommy, they'll only be here for a couple of hours,' Nan calls over the sound of

One time Jack's nan Sue actually did eat the bum out of a low-flying duck.

the video. 'You have a rest.'

'Maybe I'll just go into the kitchen . . .' I say.

'No, love, don't do that. It's chilly out there. You'll catch your death. We'll try not to bother you. I'll just get my yoga gear on.'

'But I . . .'

Nan heads off to her bedroom. The other ladies are all lined up, giggling, limbering up, windmilling arms, marching in place. They watch the yoga lady on the screen and start to exercise. Well, I think that's what it is. Exercise. They're certainly moving, and they seem to be watching the TV. It's just that their movements don't look anything like what Yoga Lady is doing.

The volume is up so loud my eardrums rattle.

'Turn it up a bit, will you, Sue,' Julie calls.

'Let's Salute the Sun,' says Yoga Lady in a calm, soothing voice.

All the oldies bend back as far as they can. Julie falls over and lands on her backside.

'Are you okay?' Sue calls as the others touch their toes.

'Yep,' Julie says, struggling to her feet and setting her glasses straight.

Now they all lunge forward, bending at the knees, one leg thrust out in front, one behind.

'Oooo, I think I just pulled a hammy,' says Sandra, the cake shop lady.

Nan emerges from the bedroom wearing a rainbow-coloured leotard. She looks like an optical illusion. Just the sight of her makes my head pound.

'We're Saluting the Sun,' Sue tells Nan. They all place their hands on the carpet, lie down then push up, bending their backs. Even over the noise of the music I can hear their spines cracking. It sounds like a sumo wrestler dancing on bubble wrap.

Part of me is fascinated that, at their age, they can stretch and twist and bend like this.

'Let's explore the Downward Dog pose,' creepy-calm Yoga Lady says, and the grannies all turn away. They bend over and point their fluorescent lycra-clad bottoms in the air directly at me. It's quite scary. I've never seen so many bottoms at the same time at close range. I feel like I'm under enemy attack. I now know how Pop felt in the war. Hang on, one of the cannons just fired – it was Sue's, the biggest of them all. I cover my nose but it's no good. This is nuclear. My cyes water. My skin starts to itch. I wait for sores to bubble up all over me. I have to get out of here.

I thought we were having an eclipse,

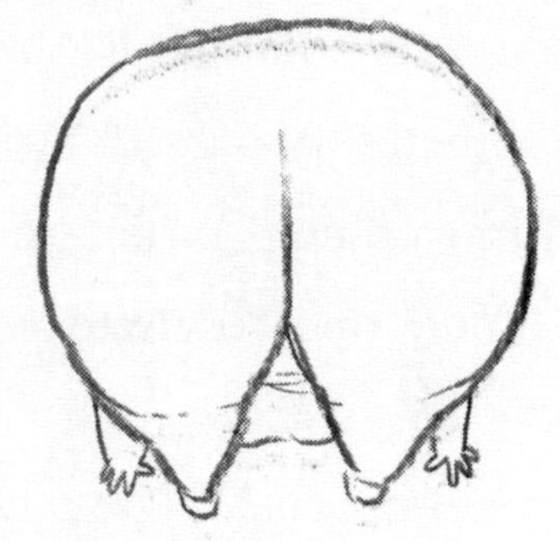

but Sue was just touching her toes.

I stand and am nearly whacked in the face by Sue's swinging arm as she rises and stretches. 'Oh, that's better,' she says.

I weave between the ladies, closing my eyes to avoid seeing anything else I might regret.

'Where are you off to, Tommy?' Nan asks.

'Just . . . I'm . . . I have to go to the toilet!' I say.

'Alright, love.'

When she turns around I slip out into the kitchen, press the door closed and lean my back against it. I take three slow, deep breaths – just like Yoga Lady said. How could something so good turn so bad so quickly? I find a blue pen next to the phone and scribble a note on a serviette.

Dear Nan,

Feeling much better. Have gone to school. Thanks for the eggs.

Love, Tom.

I drop the pen and bolt down the hall, out the back door and across Nan's yard. I jump the fence, hit the footpath and keep right on running. I imagine every step I take is onto a delete button, erasing the memories of the past 30 minutes from my mind, permanently.

I arrive at school just as the bell sounds for the end of recess. I'm so thankful to be back. I leap the fence behind the canteen, slip around the side and fall into step with the kids coming back from the top oval. We head up the stairs into the main building and, moments later, I'm sliding into my comfy orange plastic school chair, safe and sound, without a single pumpkin-soup-making, corner-lip-kissing, cheek-twisting, lycra-wearing old yoga lady in sight.

It's heaven.

Jack sits next to me. 'What's wrong? You look terrible. And is that lipstick on your face?'

I rub my cheek and notice that Jack has what looks like red drink stains at the corners of his mouth.

Miss Norrish arrives. 'Settle down, please. Exam conditions. Quiet, please!'

She moves around the classroom, handing out papers.

'It's 11.00,' I whisper to Jack. 'You've already done the exam.'

'No, we haven't.'

'It was on at 9.30,' I say.

'It's Sophie's birthday. Her mum brought in cake from the patisserie, so we had that and creaming soda under the fig tree. It was sooo good. We're doing the exam now.'

'No way,' I say.

'Yes way,' Jack replies with a sugary, cake-smelling burp.

Miss Norrish drops the ten-page maths test on my desk in front of me.

'Where were you this morning, anyway?' Jack whispers.

'Sick,' I say.

'Yeah, you look kind of sweaty and jumpy,' he tells me. 'Why'd you come back to school? Man, you must really love exams.'

Jack laughs.

I cry.

Toffee

by Anjali Dutton

My friend Anjali is super-funny. She's 11 years old and one of those people who stuff always happens to. At her last school, she had a disastrous toffee incident, and I asked her to write a story about it. This is what happened . . .

I used to believe, until yesterday, that toffee was yummy, fun and delicious – an absolute dee-light to the senses.

Now, I'm not so sure.

Look, I hadn't eaten *a lot* of toffee before.

My family are clean-living, sugar-avoiding vegetarians. Our idea of a treat is a green smoothie and a tofu-and-goji-berry cookie. Yummmmmmy!

So, yesterday . . .

It all started innocently enough. There I was at the year five get-together after school. Our teacher, Miss Green, who is perfectly nice and yet the most dreadfully nervous and uptight woman you'll ever meet, thinks we should 'get together' weekly because (as she recites A LOT), 'Class harmony is assisted by extra-curricular student–parent social interaction.'

Really? Isn't six hours all day, every day, enough? Normally our get-togethers are at the park, but it was raining so we were stuck on the classroom veranda. It was noisy – really, really, REALLLLLLY NOISYYYYYYYY! My classmates were generally misbehaving like mad, manic monkeys and sounding like badly tuned violins mixed with squeaky, un-oiled trumpets. Meanwhile, the parents were forced to chat loudly above the noise of this crazy kid orchestra about the behavioural issues of *other people's* children and the nutritional quality of other children's 'snacks to share'.

Our class has a healthy eating policy but, there, among the fruit kebabs, the dips and crackers, the vegetable crudités and the sugar/dairy/wheat-free kale muffins, was the most yummy and enticing thing ever. It was honey-golden and wildly sprinkled with hundreds and thousands, and glinted temptingly into my eyes, making my mouth water.

The parents were absolutely horrified, wondering who had dared

Here is a gluten-free, wheat-free, sugar-free, organic, vegan, basil-activated, kale and eggplant pie.

It tastes like this nine-week-old sandwich from the bottom of my bag.

to bring this toffee. One father quivered with rage: 'Why did I send my child to this school if you feed them such rubbish?' He flopped onto the wet, bindi-covered ground, splattering his organic bamboo yoga clothes with mud. He pounded his hands on the ground, sobbing, 'This is poison! I made my specialty – a triple-soaked activated almond, brussels sprout, turnip and asparagus cheesecake. I did it all myself. Who made this sugary toffee MUCK?' Tears rolling in torrents down his cheeks, he went to swipe the toffees clean off the table – but he was too late.

I yelled 'TOFFEE!' and there was a mad rush. Kids pounced from all sides. I grabbed a piece and ran towards the far corner of the playground. As I scurried across the grass I could hear adults yelling and kids being forced to give back their toffees. NO WAY that was going to happen to me. I tucked in behind a fig tree over near the creek. I slid down and sat, looking at my precious golden treasure glistening in the late afternoon light.

Then . . . I licked it. Yum! I took a tiny bite – a little sticky but still delicious. I loved it so much that I forced the whole piece into my mouth and bit down hard, expecting the toffee to shatter and dissolve on my tongue. But the toffee did not smash into smithereens; no, my teeth barely made a dent. I tried to open my mouth to chew but I couldn't. My jaw was jammed. The toffee had turned on me. My teeth were stuck like cement!

I stood and walked quickly back across the playground, feeling embarrassed and finding it slightly difficult to breathe. I climbed onto the veranda and tapped my dad on the shoulder. He was agreeing with Miss Green about the dangers of television on young minds, saying, 'We threw ours out years ago.' (Which is totally not true. We watch *Family Feud* every night, without fail.)

'Just a moment please, Anjali,' he continued. 'I agree entirely. Parents who let their children watch television should be jailed.'

I tapped his shoulder again.

'Just a *moment* please, Anjali.' He was annoyed now.

I jabbed his shoulder harder and he spun around. 'WHAT is so important that you must interrupt our very important discussion?'

'Ggggmm! Mgggmam! Lummmmgggg!' I said, which is toffee-speak for, 'My mouth is stuck!'

'Hmm?' Dad asked. 'I don't understand.'

I tried again. 'Ymmmmmi mrrrrrrrrrottthha sssssstugg!'

'What are you saying? Don't be so ridiculous, Anjali.'

'Ugghhh,' I groaned with exasperation and went into the classroom to grab a piece of paper and a pen. Leaning against the teacher's desk, I wrote, 'MY MOUTH IS STUCK

LIKE GLUE. HELP!'

I went back out onto the veranda and passed the note to Dad.

'Sorry,' he said to Miss Green before turning to me. 'Anjali, this is unacceptable. I expect you to know bett–' He read my note, looked at me and realised how serious I was.

'Excuse me for a moment,' he said to my teacher and shuffled me away from the crowd to the edge of the veranda.

'Why is your jaw stuck?' he whispered

'Muuuuumm graaarth guuum goooobie,' I explained.

He leaned in, got a grip on my nose and chin, and pulled and tugged, but he could not pry my mouth open.

'It's not one of those stupid *toffees*, is it?' he asked.

I lowered my head in shame.

He was so disappointed, and he looked around to see if anyone had heard. 'Wait right

here,' he said. Then he ran off towards our camper van.

'Gag?' I called, toffee-speak for, 'Dad?'

But he didn't look back. Where was he going? Was he embarrassed, too?

'Is everything alright, Anjali?' Miss Green called over the roar of kids and parents. She looked suspicious.

I covered my mouth, nodded and turned away. She would flip if she knew I'd glued my jaw shut with toffee. She'd have me expelled and held up as an example in the school newsletter of what happens to those guilty of sugar-related crimes. I couldn't let that happen.

Dad emerged from the van a few minutes later, carrying a steaming saucepan. He marched triumphantly through the little kids' sandpit and past the climbing equipment. As he came closer, I saw what was in the pot – a disgusting green liquid that looked like slime.

'Eeeeeeeewwwwww!' said my friend Isobel, looking over my shoulder. 'Is that, like, hot *snot*?'

Dad beamed proudly. 'Heated green smoothie.'

'Guuuuumry caaaan griii,' I said, shaking my head urgently, toffee-speak for, 'Your green smoothie is the most disgusting substance known to humankind.'

'This'll help,' he said. 'Come down here.' He grabbed my hand and pulled me off the veranda and onto the grass, out of sight.

'Okay, tip your head back,' Dad said.

I wanted to say no. I wanted to tell him

Life tips # 37

Just because you can put it in a smoothie, doesn't mean you should.

where he could stick his green smoothie. But I also kind of wanted to be able to open my mouth again.

I knew exactly what the smoothie was made of – a disgusting mix of kale, celery, rotten bananas and broccoli. Dad's 'Detox Delight'. He absolutely swears by it. He says it could 'unclog a cat's bum'! (Wow, Dad, you should totally be a poet.)

I reluctantly tilted my head back and he poured it into my mouth. It was, as usual, unearthly, outrageously atrocious! The warm green goo seeped around the edges of the toffee and drizzled down my throat. Then, when I'd swallowed almost a litre of it, a stray piece of kale-clogged celery shot up my nose.

I couldn't breathe! Panicking, I jerked my head forward. Now I couldn't breathe through my mouth *or* my nose.

'Are you okay?' Dad asked.

I turned away from him and let out the biggest sneeze EVER. The celery dislodged from my nose like a giant snot stick, and the toffee un-stuck! It flew from my mouth like a missile and, to my great horror, landed in the perfectly straightened black hair of Miss Green.

'WHAT AND WHO WAS THAT?!' she screeched, plunging her hand into her hair and getting her fingers stuck in the saliva-and-green-smoothie-covered toffee. She tried to pull it out but it wouldn't budge.

'Is this what I think it is?' she asked. 'It smells like . . . sugar! Who has been eating sugar on my veranda? I repeat: *WHO has been eating sugar on my veranda?*' Miss Green had gone from white with shock to red with rage.

Now she was turning an unattractive shade of purple.

Dad grabbed my hand firmly and we dashed past the climbing equipment, through the sandpit, and made a beeline for our camper van.

As we scampered away, I heard Miss Green shrieking: 'Anjali and Scott Dutton, get back here right now!'

Interview With Myself in a Bathroom Mirror

I figure, since I'm going to be rich and famous and stuff, I'd better get used to being interviewed. Nobody's knocking down my door for an exclusive – yet – so I thought, *Who better to interview me than . . . me?* I often talk to myself in the mirror, using a toothbrush as a microphone. So, this time, I recorded it. Check it out.

Me: So, tell me, Tom, do you have any pets?

Me: 'Bando, a dog.'

Me: Fascinating. Can Bando do any special tricks?

Me: 'He can roll over.'

Me: Really?

Me: 'No. He can't do anything.'

Me: Favourite food?

Me: 'Meaty Bites.'

Me: No, I mean *your* favourite food.

Me: 'Oh. Mexican. Tacos. Fish tacos. And Ben & Jerry's New York Super Fudge Chunk ice-cream.'

Me: Colour?

Me: 'Always inside the lines.'

Me: No, I mean, what's your favourite colour?

Me: 'Um. Blue.'

Me: If you could be any animal, what would you be?

Me: 'A hippo. Kind of cute-looking but unexpectedly deadly.'

Me: Have you ever kissed a girl?

Me: 'Yes, but not by choice.'

Me: Do you like pie?

Me: 'Yes, I do like pie. And please stop asking such weird questions.

Blueberry pie, by the way. And Mexican.'

Me: What's your favourite joke?

Me: 'I have four.

- What's invisible and smells like carrots? Bunny farts.
- Why did the toilet paper jump off the cliff? It was desperate to get to the bottom.
- Where do you find a tortoise with no legs? Right where you left it.
- Why did the student eat his homework? Because the teacher told him it was a piece of cake.'

Me: Tell us about your new book.

Me: 'Well, it has an interview in it where I interview myself in a bathroom mirror.'

Me: Wow, very original. What did you ask yourself?

Me: 'Oh, you know, just stuff.'

Me: What sort of stuff?

Me: 'Stuff like, "Do you have any pets?"'

Me: Yes, Bando, a dog.

Me: 'Fascinating. Can Bando do any special tricks?'

Me: He can roll over.

Me: 'Really?'

Me: No. He can't do anything.

Me: 'Favourite food?'

Me: Meaty Bites.

Me: 'No, I mean *your* favourite food.'

Send me an interview with yourself and maybe I can put it on my blog or in my next book: TheTomWeekly@gmail.com

Tom Weekly
– the EXCLUSIVE interview!

The First Kiss

Tonight will be the best night of my life – the night I get to kiss Sasha, the cutest and smartest girl in Australia, for the first time ever, on stage, in front of everyone.

'Tom, have you died in there?' Mum calls, pounding on the bathroom door. 'We have to go.'

I saw at my teeth with my toothbrush. This is the fourth time I've brushed this afternoon. Not to mention the litre of mouthwash and two packets of mints I've polished off. I've been waiting to kiss Sasha since I was six years old, and if my breath smells like the garlic that Mum put in the pasta sauce tonight, this may be the first and last time we kiss. This could destroy my plan for me and Sasha to get married and have three kids and a labradoodle and a house overlooking the ocean with secret passages and revolving bookcases. (I have this all laid out in a scrapbook hidden in the trapdoor under the rug in the middle of my bedroom floor. Not that I'm weird or creepy.)

Sasha AND me . . .

FOREVER!

I wrote the school play *Here Comes Mr Wolf* with me in mind for the lead role – a young wolf about the same age as Sasha's Red Riding Hood. The first half retells the fairy-tale of Little Red Riding Hood, up to the point when Mr Wolf is dressed as Grandma and is about to eat poor little Red. The second half is a courtroom drama where Mr Wolf goes on trial for murder, breaks down in tears, apologises for eating Grandma and regurgitates the old woman whole (which takes some serious acting skills to pull off). Red Riding Hood is so thankful and feels so sorry for poor Mr Wolf that she takes him in her arms and kisses him. They fall in love, Mr Wolf promises to become a vegetarian, and they live happily ever after.

Sasha and I haven't kissed at all in rehearsals. We want to save it for the performance, so that it seems really real, since the Wolf and Little Red have never kissed before either. If we've been kissing each other's faces off in rehearsals, maybe the audience won't believe it on the night.

Actually, that's not true. I wanted to kiss in rehearsals but Sasha suggested we wait. I didn't want to seem desperate, so I said, 'Yes. Definitely. Good idea. Let's wait.' But I didn't mean it. We've been rehearsing for a month

and I almost died from not kissing her. ('Not Kissing Sasha' is an official disease. Look it up. I broke out in a rash, got the shivers and my tongue swelled up like a sausage roll.)

The worst part is that I couldn't tell anyone how desperate I was to kiss her. If I'd mentioned it to Jack, he would have told everyone. And, anyway, he's fallen in love with Stella Holling, the girl who's been in love with *me* since second grade. 'Fallen in love' might be a bit strong. Let's just say that Stella has turned her attention towards Jack and he isn't complaining. He thinks we should go on a double-date – me and Sasha and him and Stella. Never. Going. To. Happen. I'm allergic to Stella.

'I'm going to the car, Tom. You're on stage in 45 minutes. Move your butt!' Mum slams the front door.

I set the toothbrush down next to the sink and gaze into my own eyes. In my mind, they are Sasha's eyes. She is staring back at me, wearing a red hood. I lean in slowly and kiss the mirror tenderly. (I need to practise. The truth is that I've never kissed a girl before. Unless you count the hundred times Stella Holling has tricked me into kissing her. Which I choose not to.)

The mirror tastes a bit like window cleaner, so I stop kissing myself. I wipe all the slobber off and I'm ready.

Mum beeps the horn. Showtime.

It's chaos backstage. Chorus kids are singing warm-up scales. Stage crew are making final adjustments to the set and props. Actors are walking in circles, muttering their lines.

Mr Skroop, the director of this evening's performance, barks orders to the troops: 'TEN minutes till curtain, everybody! Band members still backstage should find their positions in the orchestra pit IMMEDIATELY. Nicholas, that's hardly an appropriate use of a trombone!'

As well as being the play's director, Skroop is our Deputy Principal and my next-door neighbour. He is tall and skinny with brown, gappy teeth and an attitude.

I peek around the edge of the curtain to see the audience filling up the hall. Last time I performed here was at the Christmas concert, when Jack and I played our world-premiere show as The Clappers. We totally crushed it. Tonight feels different, though. The stakes are higher because of Sasha. And because Mr Wolf is the biggest role of my life – the *only* role of my life. I let the curtain fall back into place. I breathe into my hand and sniff. Still minty but thick with garlic, proving my theory that my mother is trying to ruin my life.

'Wow, you look amazing, Tom,' says my teacher, Miss Norrish. She tweaks the nose at the end of my long-snouted wolf mask.

'Thanks. Have you seen Sasha at all? We need to go through our lines.'

'No, I haven't. Are you still worried about throwing up Grandma?' Miss Norrish asks. 'I think they've fixed the smoke machine. It should be fine.'

'Uh-oh,' I whisper. Mr Skroop approaches. He despises me and would never have given me the role of Mr Wolf if I hadn't written the play. Or if anyone else in the school had auditioned.

'I'll leave you to it,' Miss Norrish says, scurrying away.

'Weekly, I have some news for you,' Skroop says.

'Yes, Mr Skroop?'

'Your girlfriend is sick. She can't perform tonight.'

'What?!'

'Sasha's understudy will be playing the role of Red Riding Hood this evening.'

The understudy is the person who plays the role if the main actor is sick, and I know *exactly* who that understudy is.

'No! That's not possible.'

'It is possible. And it is happening. Curtain in six minutes.' He turns to go.

'What's wrong with Sasha?' I ask as he walks away.

'Food poisoning, apparently.' He turns and

looks over his shoulder at me in a way that makes me feel as though *he* poisoned her. Although, in fairness, Skroop always looks like he just poisoned someone, so it's probably nothing to worry about.

I stand there in the wings of the stage, people crisscrossing all around, but I feel so alone, like one of those guys whose wife-to-be runs away on the wedding day, leaving him standing at the altar.

Sasha's understudy appears from behind one of the curtain wings. She is smiling and wearing Sasha's red hood and chequered red-and-white dress. This makes my blood boil.

'Hello, Wolfy,' she says.

This is not happening, this is not happening, this is not happening.

My breathing is tight and I feel light-headed. I think I might faint.

'Hello, Stella,' I say through gritted teeth.

Stella Holling, the girl who constantly tricks, swindles and bribes me into kissing her, is Sasha's understudy.

'Too bad about Sasha,' she says, but her eyes are saying, *Kissy-kissyyy*. 'Oh well, not to worry. We'll just have to do the best we can. Do you want to run through our lines? Do you want to practise the –'

'NO! I do not want to practise the . . .' I can't even say the word. I promised myself I'd never let Stella kiss me again. I stare at her, wishing my eyes were toxic slime-shooters. 'I don't want to practise anything with you. The only thing I want to practise with you is running in the opposite direction.'

'That's no way for the playwright and star of the show to speak to his leading lady,' she says. She leans in and whispers, 'This is our destiny, Tommy.'

I shudder. 'This is *not* our destiny, Stella. This is what's known as a sick, twisted joke. And aren't you meant to be Jack's girlfriend?'

She laughs and throws her head back. 'Is that what he told you?'

I shrug.

'I could never fall in love with another man, Tommy. You're my true love.'

I gulp. It feels like I'm swallowing an emu egg.

'What's that smell, by the way?' she asks. 'Have you been eating something interesting?'

'Yes,' I say with a slowly spreading grin. '*Garlic*.'

'Oooooo,' she says. 'I *adore*

garlic. It makes me think of my grandma's pizzas. Some people hate the smell, but I think it's yummy-yummy-yummy. Anyway, I'll see you out there, husband.'

'I'm not your husband, Stella.'

'Not yet. But you will be . . . *Wolfy*.' She purrs like a cat, blows me a kiss with those scary, sea-creature lips and vanishes behind the curtain.

I take three deep breaths.

I would usually get angry about this and complain about how unfair it is. I'd say, 'Why does this always happen to me?' But I need to just accept that this is my fate. Stella Holling is going to haunt me for the rest of my days. Why fight it? We might as well get married now. Who cares that she sends shivers down my spine? Who cares that I would rather kiss a baboon's bottom than her? Who cares that it's illegal to get married when you're in primary school?

'Three minutes!' Skroop shouts from the backstage corridor.

Jack appears out of nowhere, carrying an axe. He is playing the role of the jolly woodcutter, but he doesn't look all that jolly right now.

'I'm so glad to see you,' I say. 'Guess what?'

'I've heard,' Jack snarls. 'You'd better not lay a single lip on Stella.'

'Huh?'

'She's my girl.'

'Your *girl*?' I say. 'She's not a *girl*. She's –'

'If I find out you poisoned Sasha so that Stella could play Red Riding Hood just so you could kiss her –'

'As if I'd want to kiss Stella! She's already kissed me, like, a bazillion times! And she's so . . . *Stella*.'

'What do you mean by that?' Jack asks. 'What does, "She's so *Stella*" mean exactly? I oughta punch you right now.'

I take him by the shoulders and shake him. 'Wake up! Do you even know who Stella Holling is? She's the devil and Voldemort and classical music all rolled into one!'

I think Jack has tricked himself into liking Stella. For the past few weeks he has had a girlfriend called Aurora, a strict vegan (which means she doesn't eat animals in any form, ever). Jack pretended to be vegan, too – until Aurora caught him stuffing a meat pie with sauce into his gob behind the canteen last Friday. Aurora dumped him on the spot. I think he's using Stella to get back at her.

'Just keep your big, disgusting, slobbery jaws off her,' he says, raising his axe. 'I don't want to have to chop anything off.'

I wince. The axe is made of cardboard and aluminium foil, but it still looks quite scary.

'Break a leg.' Jack turns and goes.

I slump to the floor, my back against the brick wall of the hall, head in my hands. The best night of my life is now the worst. Jack will kill me if I kiss Stella. Mr Skroop will kill me if I don't, because it'll ruin the play. I may die if I kiss Stella again. Stella is desperate to kiss me, but if Sasha hears that I've been kissing Stella, she may never go out with me. I can't win!

'Positions, everybody!' Skroop calls. 'First positions!'

The actors take their places in the forest set. Red Riding Hood and her mother are inside a little cottage. I'm hidden behind a

Things I would rather do than kiss Stella Holling #129

tree. The tree is played by Brent Bunder, the biggest kid in my school. His armpits smell like two dead possums.

'Ha!' the tree whispers to me. 'You've got to kiss Holling.'

The curtains part, the audience claps and cheers, and the play begins with Stella's opening line.

'Oh, please, Mother. I so wish to go and see Grandmama.'

That's not even what I wrote! She's changing the script and ruining my masterpiece with her terrible acting.

In spite of Stella's performance, the first act of *Here Comes Mr Wolf* goes off without a hitch. The audience laughs in all the right spots, no one forgets their lines, and I almost get to eat Stella. I slink offstage to lots of back-patting and 'That was so good!' and 'You were great!'

But I don't feel great. I head for the

corridor at the back of the stage.

'Where are you going?' Skroop snaps.

'I need to go to the toilet.'

'Well, hurry! We only have a couple of minutes while we change the set for the second act, and then we're back on.'

I head into the bathroom, flip my wolf mask up on my head, twist the tap on and flood my face with cold water. It feels good. I stand and wipe my eyes. I look in the mirror. I'm staring at a different guy than the one I saw at home earlier tonight. I look like I've been to war. Some kind of war where the troops get to dress up in wild animal costumes. I've aged about nine years worrying about kissing Stella.

Maybe I should just run. I'll slip out the back door of the hall, bolt across the top oval, down the main street and catch a train to . . . Wagga Wagga.

Just then I hear a small voice. At first I

think it's in my mind. But then I hear the voice again: 'Help!'

I listen harder.

'Heeeelp!' says the tiny voice.

I know this is weird, but it sounds a bit like . . . Sasha.

The door screeches open. 'Back on stage, Weekly. Now! One minute till curtain.'

'Mr Skroop! I think I can hear Sasha. It sounds like she's in trouble. Listen.'

'We don't have time –'

'Please, just listen a moment.'

Skroop sighs. We wait, listening for ten, maybe 15 seconds. I can hear him breathing noisily through his mouth.

We hear nothing.

'Let's move it.'

'No, really, I –'

'NOW!' Skroop booms from the deep, dark pit inside him.

I head out of the bathroom and into the

corridor, my ears still tuned. 'It sounded like it was coming from there,' I say, pointing to a door with a black-and-white label that reads 'Storage Room'.

'GO!'

I jump and move quickly through the wings and out onto the stage. The set has been changed to the courtroom. I pull my wolf mask down over my face and take the stand.

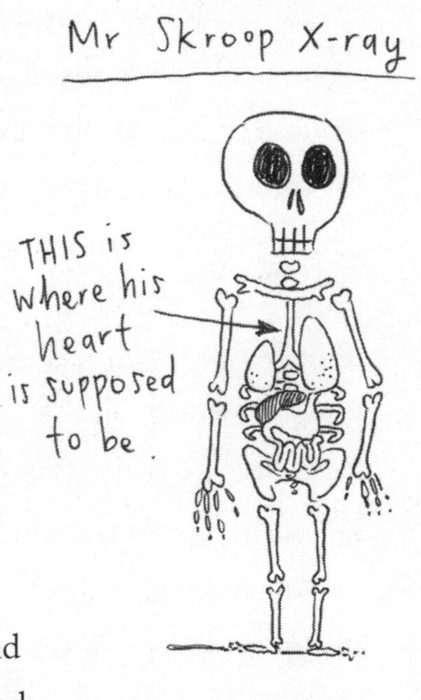

The curtains open. The audience claps and we dive into the second act of the play. I churn through my lines with no feeling at all. I can actually see audience members, mostly dads, asleep. Those who aren't asleep are shuffling in their stiff plastic chairs. Before I know it, I am regurgitating Grandma in a breathtaking explosion of special effects, smoke-machine wizardry and strobe lighting. A few of the dads wake up.

Stella cuddles Grandma, wipes off some of the wolf saliva and stares at me with her devilish, creepy brown eyes. Then she moves in for the kiss. Jack, standing behind her, pretends to sharpen his cardboard axe and gives me not-so-jolly woodcutter eyes of death. In my imagination I can hear Sasha quietly calling, 'Help! Help!'

Stella says, 'Oh, Wolfy, thank you. I don't know how to repay you.'

The audience says, 'Ooooooooooooo,' sitting up, knowing what's coming.

Don't! I think. *Don't repay me! I'd be happy to regurgitate your grandmother a thousand times. No payment necessary.*

The garlic smell of my breath is making me sick, but Stella, just centimetres from my face, inhales it like French perfume. Her sea-creature lips are dangerously close to mine, and I'm staring into her galaxy of sweaty freckles when I hear the loudest shriek I have ever heard. Stella and I turn. So does everyone else on stage, and in the audience.

It's Sasha. She's running across the stage towards us. Skroop, her parents and Miss Norrish are chasing her. Sasha's eyes are wild, her hair is a mess. She launches herself through the air towards me and Stella, her arms outstretched.

'That's my wolf!' she screams, then collides with Stella in a slap of skin and a crunch of bones, tackling her to the floor. Stella hits the stage and does not move – she's been knocked out cold. Jack drops his cardboard axe and runs to her side.

Sasha peels herself off the ground, stands and looks me in the eyes. She tears off my wolf mask and leans in towards me. I know

The kiss scene turned out to be more like a scene from **THE MATRIX**

that I must be dreaming because this sort of thing does not happen to me in real life. I never get the girl. Only, this feels so real. Sasha's soft lips press against mine. If this is a dream, I never want it to end.

The crowd goes wild. They must think that Stella being knocked out was all part of the show. They stand and clap and hoot and stomp their feet. They think it's the greatest ending to a play in the history of theatre, but I could never write something this good.

Sasha pulls back suddenly and the crowd settles down. The kiss is over.

She whispers, 'Have you been eating garlic, Tom?'

I don't want to lie to her, so I say, 'Yes. Sorry. It's Mum's sauce.'

She stares at me. The crowd stares at us.

Sasha smiles and whispers, 'I don't care.' Then she kisses me again, right there in front of everyone we know. The crowd goes crazy again. We continue kissing until the curtains close and the house lights come on.

Next day at school Stella is given a week-long lunchtime detention for locking Sasha in a cupboard at the back of the storage room and making up the story about food poisoning.

In the playground, kids whistle at me and Sasha. They ask if we're girlfriend and boyfriend now. I say, 'Maybe' and 'I guess so.' Sasha says, 'No.' So we agree to disagree. But I figure that even if Sasha and I don't get married and have three kids and a labradoodle and a house overlooking the ocean with secret passages and revolving bookcases, we'll always have that kiss – the one time in my life when everything went even better than I had planned.

The Good Boy

Lately I've been getting into trouble for lots of little things. I mean, adults are way too sensitive. You break two or three windows in a week and your mum gets *so* upset. You get caught passing a note in class five or six times a lesson and your teacher goes crazy. You stretch the truth a little when it comes to your involvement in a particular incident involving fireworks and a cat, and your next-door neighbour gets *so* worked up about it.

No video games. Detention. Pocket money suspended until further notice.

It stinks.

Things that don't go together #521

But adults have been around for thousands of years – maybe more – and I'm probably not going to be able to change their weird little ways during my short childhood, so I figure I'll try playing by their rules – for today, at least. If I can make it through an entire day without doing a single thing wrong, maybe I'll try it again tomorrow. Over time, if I can allow adults to turn me into a robot with no feelings or originality, and I do exactly what they say all the time, maybe I'll get my video games and pocket money back. Maybe I won't have to spend my lunchtimes reciting times tables outside Skroop's office, and I'll live happily ever after.

Maybe.

It begins today. Starting right now, I'm going to be good for an entire 24 hours.

I pull my bedroom door open and step out into the world. I look both ways. Nothing. I'm doing well. It's five seconds past 7.00 am and nothing has gone wrong yet. I turn left and head down the hall towards the kitchen, ready for anything.

'Morning, Mum!' I say, trying to sound as chirpy as I can without making her suspicious.

'Hi, Tom. Can you please empty the dishwasher?'

I stand and stare at her as she sits on the couch in her work clothes and fluffy pink slippers. She's straightening her hair, eating buttered toast and watching a morning show . . . and she wants me to empty the dishwasher. Why should I be working like a dog while she's watching a story about a celebrity wedding in Las Vegas?

'*Tom?*'

'Yes?'

'Dishwasher. Now. Bus goes in less than half an hour. Move it.'

My instinct is to say, *You're a bit snappy this morning!* or *Why can't Tanya empty it?* or *Comfortable, are you? Can I get you another cushion?*

But I don't. I remember the promise I made to myself 37 seconds ago – I'm going to be good for an entire day. It can't be that hard.

'Okay, Mum,' I say with a forced grin. 'No problem. Just let me know if you need anything else.'

'You've woken in a nice mood,' she says. 'What's wrong? You've been so horrible recently.'

Horrible? She actually uses the word 'horrible' to describe me, one of the nicest people I know. But instead of getting annoyed I say, 'Sorry, Mum, I know I've been a little bit difficult to live with. I'm doing my best to turn things around.'

She looks at me and frowns. 'You're not sick, are you?'

I choose to ignore her rudeness. 'No, I feel great!' And I sort of do. This whole 'being good' thing isn't as hard as I thought. You just have to say 'yes' all the time.

'Yes,' I whisper under my breath, practising my new mantra. 'Yes. Sure. No problem.' I can do that for 24 hours.

I turn and see my sister, Tanya, sitting at the island bench that separates the lounge room from the kitchen. She's slurping down a bowl of Froot Loops. She opens her mouth and shows me the soggy rainbow mash of cereal on her tongue.

'Mu-um!' I say. It's out before I can stop myself.

'Don't dob, Tom,' Mum tells me.

I stop. I breathe, slowly, deeply. I remember

that I am a robot and I must say 'yes' to everything my adult overlords tell me to do. I continue past her to empty the dishwasher. I lean down to pick up the cutlery basket, and Tanya says, needling me, 'Don't you have a French assignment due today, Tom?'

I clench my jaw and squeeze the handle of the cutlery basket so tight that the forks and spoons start to jingle from the earthquake inside me. I pray that, somehow, Mum is too involved in the celebrity wedding to have heard Tanya, but no such luck.

'That's right,' Mum says. 'Aren't you supposed to cook us a French dessert or something?'

I stay low, beneath the level of the bench, so that she can't see me baring my teeth, or the saliva dripping down my chin.

'Miss Norrish says it's not even an assessment task,' I say, trying to keep my voice even. 'It's just if we want to do it.'

'That's not what the assignment sheet on the fridge says,' Mum tells me.

'It's too late now. It's due today,' I say.

'Oh, good, you can cook it for us this afternoon and submit the assignment online tonight,' she says, standing and switching off the TV.

I peek over the island bench. 'Yes, Mum.'

'Don't "Yes, Mum" me. If I have another note home about a late assignment, I'm donating your organs to science. Finish emptying the dishwasher, eat your breakfast and go brush your teeth.'

I love how she casually mentions that she's going to have my heart, lungs and kidneys removed, but she still wants to keep my teeth in tiptop condition.

Mum puts her plate on the bench and heads for the front door. 'See you this afternoon. Tanya, do you want a lift?'

'Yes, thanks, Mum,' Tanya says sweetly, then turns to me and whispers, slowly and huskily: 'Su-u-ucked in.'

I want to throw a fork at her . . . but I am being good for an entire day, so I'll have to wait till tomorrow.

They leave. Tanya slams the door. I growl and sit on a stool at the kitchen bench. My life stinks. This whole 'being good' thing is overrated. Bando, sitting under the bench, licks my hand. I give him the crust from Mum's toast. He winks at me and yawns excitedly.

'I wish you could do my assignment for me,' I say to him.

He gives me that goofy, black-lipped smile of his, as though he thinks it's a really good idea. Bando thinks everything I say is a good idea. I scruff him on the neck.

For the assignment we have to make a French dessert for our family, photograph it and write a journal entry about the process, but I'm a terrible cook. I once burnt a smoothie.

I finish unpacking the dishwasher, eat breakfast and brush my teeth. I still have five minutes till the bus goes, so I raid the pantry for ingredients. I don't even *know* any French desserts. I try to remember what Miss Norrish said. Soufflé? I wonder what's in a soufflé. I pull out anything that looks slightly dessert-y

– cinnamon, rice bubbles, sugar, oats, vanilla essence, hundreds and thousands, and a big bag of carob powder. I take a couple of pears from the fruit bowl, sit them on the kitchen bench next to the rest, grab my bag and head out the door. I'll work out what I'm going to make at school.

It turns out to be the worst day ever. The one day I try to be good, everything bad happens. First lesson is barn dancing for P. E. I'm paired with Stella Holling and have to dance with her for an hour. I try to keep her at arm's length, but she keeps me in a death grip and manages to kiss me three times – once on the left shoulder and once on each ear. I have a massive wedgie the whole time from the underpants Mum shrank in the dryer, and because of Stella's wrestling hold I can't pick it out.

In the afternoon we have 'buddies', where each of us is teamed up with a kindy kid for an hour. I have a kid named Braden Chambers. I accidentally drop him when he asks me to catch him off the monkey bars, so he bites me really hard on the hand. I want to pinch him, but you know what? I don't. Even though I know the world is out to get me, I keep my cool. I don't flip out. I say 'yes' to it all.

By the time I'm on the bus I've done eight-and-a-half hours of the good boy routine. In five hours I'll be in bed. I'm totally going to make it across the finish line.

Or so I think.

I know something's up as soon as I open the front door. For starters, Bando's inside. Bando should not be inside. I was supposed to put him out before I went to school. He licks me and wags his tail and bolts around the lounge room like a maniac.

The second thing I notice is that the ingredients I placed on the kitchen bench are no longer there. The boxes and bags are all over the floor, but they're empty.

'Bando,' I say in a low voice. He stops running around like a maniac. 'Did you eat all the ingredients for my assignment?'

He lowers his head and stares at the floor.

It occurs to me that if Bando has eaten that much food, he's probably done something else, too. The first rule of dog ownership: what goes in, must come out. I search the kitchen and lounge room floors, the bathroom, Tanya's room . . . and then I look in my room.

And there it is. A very large pile of poo coiled in the centre of my rug.

'BANDO!' I shout, and he slumps to the floor in my doorway.

The poo is laid in a perfect, tall spiral, like a chocolate soft-serve ice-cream. I pray that it hasn't leaked through the rug and into the

trapdoor where I keep all my banned foods, comics and best scabs. I have an unwrapped pineapple doughnut in there at the moment. I flick on the light and slowly approach. I kneel down next to the poo and inspect it, wondering what I'm going to use to remove it.

You know what's really strange? It actually doesn't smell too bad. In fact, it kind of smells . . . sweet. I use my hand to waft the aroma towards my nose. It's sort of cinnamon-y, with a hint of vanilla and the freshness of pear. Up close, it looks shiny and fluffy, like the chocolate mousse we had from the French patisserie on Jonson St on Mum's birthday.

French patisserie, I repeat in my mind.

Chocolate mousse.

'Mousse au chocolat' is a French dessert.

I saw it in a library book at lunchtime. Only this one's made with carob instead of chocolate, which is lucky because doesn't chocolate make dogs really sick?

If I can, somehow, scoop this pile up and get it onto a plate, maybe I can photograph it and say that I made chocolate mousse. I'm not going to make my family eat it or anything, but if I take the photos and write the journal entry, I'll tell Mum it was so delicious that I ate it all myself. I'm pretty sure she won't mind, as long as the assignment is submitted.

Tanya will be home soon, so there's no time to waste. I run to the kitchen, grab the wide spatula thing that Mum uses for pizzas, take a big, white plate from the top cupboard above the fridge and extract the 'mousse' in one clean swoop, leaving almost no trace of it on my rug. I slide it onto the centre of the plate and . . . it looks *amazing*. I take it out to the kitchen, place it on the bench, spray a little whipped cream on the side, plop three frozen raspberries on top and – *boom!* – my assignment is almost done.

'Good boy,' I say to Bando. 'Who knew you were a chef?!'

He pants happily and smiles.

I place a spoon on the edge of the plate and take 17 photos of my *mousse au chocolat de Bando* from various angles before I hear a rattle at the front door and it swings wide. I dive in front of my doggy dessert and stand up straight, just as Tanya walks in.

'Hi!' I say a little too eagerly.

She glares at me, blows a tiny gum bubble, pops it and says, 'Shut up, reject,' and slams the front door. She trudges across the lounge room, past the couch, past me. I inch sideways as she goes by, trying to keep my body between her and my French assignment.

She stops. 'What are you doing?'

'Nothing.'

'Why are you acting strange?'

'I'm not.'

'You are *seriously* the weirdest brother in the world.'

'Thanks,' I say, hoping we can wrap up this conversation ASAP.

She moves off towards the hallway and I shuffle a little to the left. She stops. I stop. She moves. I move. She turns and shoves me in the shoulder, pushing me out of the way, revealing what's sitting on the bench.

'What's that?'

'Nothing,' I say.

'Is that what you made for French?'

'No.'

'Is it?'

'Sort of.'

'You mean "yes"?' she asks.

'Well, not exactly.'

She drops her bag on the floor. 'Give me some.'

'No,' I say. She moves to grab the plate and I block her. 'I've still got to photograph it and –'

'Give it to me now or I'll tell Mum you ate the whole packet of emergency Tim Tams off the top of her wardrobe.'

I scowl at Tanya. It's true. I did do that. Two days ago. How can you stop at just one? Or seven? I'm annoyed that she knows. Mum is very, very protective of those biscuits. But if I give Tanya a taste of Bando's special dessert, it will ruin all the good work I've done today.

I've lasted nine whole hours without doing a single bad thing. I still have 15 hours to go. Am I really prepared to throw it all away just to see my sister eat dog poo in front of me?

Possibly.

A good boy would throw it in the bin. A good boy would drop the plate on the floor and make it seem like an accident. A good boy would run out the back door screaming, 'FIRE!' and chuck it on the compost heap. The question I have to ask myself is: Am I a good boy? Or am I evil?

'Okay,' I say, and I move aside. 'You can try it.'

I guess I must be evil.

Tanya moves towards it. 'That actually looks good. You suck at cooking. You sure you didn't buy this?'

'Yep. I'm sure,' I say. 'Definitely didn't buy it.'

She leans down towards the plate and sniffs it.

'What's in it?' she asks. 'It smells amazing.'

'Secret recipe,' I say.

'It smells like chocolate and . . .'

'Cinnamon?' I say.

'Yeah.'

'Hint of vanilla?' I suggest.

'Totally.'

'Freshness of pear?'

'Exactly!' she agrees.

She dips the tip of her pinkie into the pile.

'Wow, it's got rice bubbles in it. I love rice bubbles.'

She raises it to her face, sniffs it again and

I feel myself flinch. My face screws up. Even though it's Tanya, I know this is wrong. I really should say something. She puts her pinkie between her lips, tastes it, swirls it around with her tongue, smacks her lips together . . . I wait for her to scream, to clutch her throat, scrape her tongue or vomit, but she does none of these things. Instead, she says, 'Mmmm, delicious. A bit rich and earthy, but nice. And warm, too. Did you really make this?'

I shrug and flick a look down at Bando, who is gazing up at Tanya, his head tilted to one side. I don't think he's ever seen a human eat his poo before. This thought almost makes me explode with laughter, but I manage to turn it into a cough.

'What?' Tanya asks, immediately suspicious. 'Did you buy it?'

'No,' I say. 'All made from ingredients in the pantry.'

She maintains eye contact with me as she

picks up the spoon from the edge of the plate and digs it in. Not a small scoop but a large one this time.

'Maybe you shouldn't –' I begin.

'Maybe you shouldn't interrupt me when I'm eating,' she says.

She dips the spoonful into the cream and delicately places a raspberry on top with her fingers. Then she moves it slowly towards her mouth, grinning, teasing me, proud to be eating my delicious, rice-bubbly, cinnamon-y, chocolate mousse right in front of me.

My lips quiver and a laugh roars up my throat. I try to choke it down, but I can't stop it. It screams out of me, burning the back of my throat and finishing with a snort.

Tanya stops. 'What?'

Should I tell her? It's one thing to let your sister eat poo. It's another thing to tell her what it was. I should stop now. She demanded to eat the mousse. There's nothing I could have done. But to tell her would be bad. It would totally wreck my 24-hour goal to be good, but I may never have a chance like this again. The two sides of my brain – the good and the evil – do battle.

Tell her.

Don't say a word.

Do it.

Don't do it.

Be evil.

Be a good boy.

Nuts.

'Do you know what you're eating?' I ask.

'Duh. Chocolate mousse.'

I shake my head.

'What?' A finger of fear pokes her.

'Not chocolate mousse.'

'What then?' she asks.

'Something special,' I say, almost in a whisper.

'What?' she asks, resting the spoon on the

plate with a tiny *clink*. 'Did you put dirt in it? If you did –'

'No,' I say. 'Not dirt.' My lips quiver under the weight of the laughter I'm trying to keep inside. 'Let's just say Bando and I made that dessert *together*.'

She looks down at Bando, then up at me, and a look of terror washes over her face, turning her skin from olive to white. I will never forget that look as long as I live.

'Is it . . .?' she asks.

I nod slowly.

Tanya drops the plate on the floor and it explodes into pieces, spattering the wall with the remaining 'mousse'. She runs along the hall to the bathroom, shrieking, and flips up the lid of the toilet. 'I'm telling Mum,' she screams between barfs. 'You are *so* dead!'

I laugh hysterically, and Bando and I run through the kitchen and out the back door. I howl great, big, heaving chunks of laughter, despite having epically failed my 24-hour experiment. It will be a long, long time till I get my Xbox and pocket money back. I've also proven to myself that I cannot be good for even one single day.

In all the excitement Bando poops in the corner of the yard, laying another perfect soft-serve spiral of *mousse au chocolat de Bando*, and this makes me fall down on the grass, laughing harder than ever before. I plead with myself to stop. It hurts my belly. Bando comes over and licks my face. I sit up and, when the laughter finally eases, I crawl over to the back steps and sit on the lowest one, looking out into the yard, Bando sitting next to me.

'Do you think it was worth it?' I ask

him, and he smiles that goofy, black-lipped smile at me. 'I guess I'll try being a good boy again tomorrow.'

He yawns excitedly.

My tummy groans and I realise that I'm starving. I haven't eaten a thing since lunchtime. My eyes drift towards the still-steaming pile that Bando has left in the corner of the yard. Cinnamon-y. Vanilla-y. Freshness of pear.

Surely one little taste couldn't hurt.

Nits For Sale

'Get your nits! Two dollars per infection. Get your nits!'

'Not so loud,' I whisper to Jack. 'Miss Norrish is on duty, just over there.'

Miss Norrish is the best teacher I've ever had. She lets us chew gum on Fridays, she does roller derby on the weekend, and she once taught us for the entire day dressed as a llama to raise money for charity. But I'm not sure she'd approve of our latest harebrained business scheme.

'Sorry,' Jack says, not lowering his voice at all. 'Get your nits! Guaranteed day off school or your money back!'

We're down behind the school hall, near the bottom oval, and we have a growing line of customers snaking all the way over to the bubblers.

At this morning's assembly, Mr Skroop, the Deputy Principal, announced, 'Any child caught with head lice in tomorrow morning's annual inspection under the fig tree in the middle of the playground will be sent home *immediately*.'

As soon as he said it I looked across at Lewis Snow, one of my best friends, and I knew that he would be going home, possibly for life. Lewis has thousands of nits living in his wild blond afro. He's never had a haircut. Lewis has had nits for so long he has a nit retirement village behind his left ear. A week ago, I swear I saw a head louse in a little rocking chair back there.

I was so jealous that Lewis would get

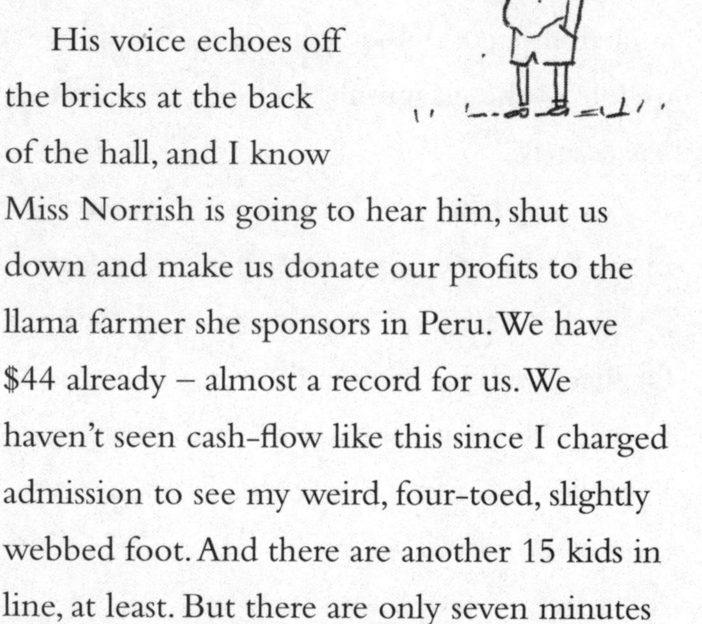

off school, and I knew everybody else would be feeling the same way. The idea popped into my head fully formed: we'll open a Nit Shop.

'Get your nits!' Jack shouts.

His voice echoes off the bricks at the back of the hall, and I know Miss Norrish is going to hear him, shut us down and make us donate our profits to the llama farmer she sponsors in Peru. We have $44 already – almost a record for us. We haven't seen cash-flow like this since I charged admission to see my weird, four-toed, slightly webbed foot. And there are another 15 kids in line, at least. But there are only seven minutes till lunchtime is over.

'We don't need any more customers,' I say.

'Let's stop while we're ahead. Get it? A head? No? Okay.'

I take Nikki's two dollars and smoosh her head against Lewis's. She winces at the feeling of being invaded by the louse army. I can actually see her fresh, white scalp being infested by the six-legged mini-beasts. They begin to feast. A small amount of vomit rises in my throat. I decide there's no way I'm giving myself nits, even if it means missing out on a day off. By the time Nikki stands up she's already scratching like mad.

Jonah Flem steps up next.

'Don't you already have nits?' I ask him, taking his two dollars.

'Yeah,' he says, 'but I figure the combo of my nits and Lewis's might create some kind of super-nit that can never be exterminated. I'll have the rest of my life off school.' He grins a lopsided grin and I smoosh their heads together.

'Can you guys hurry?' Lewis says. 'I feel like a cow being milked for my nits. And you'd better not be squishing any of them. These nits are on loan. I want them back next week.'

Lewis is the world's greatest – and only – lice lover.

By the time the bell rings we've made $74 – a new record! Lewis takes 50 per cent for providing the product. Jack and I split the rest, so I get $18.50.

'Nice work,' Jack says. We high-five and start to head off to class when Miss Norrish appears around the corner of the hall. She looks on edge. My heart pounds and I slip the cash into my pocket.

'Sorry, Miss Norrish, we're just coming now. We –'

'I know what you've been doing,' she says.

The words are like a knife in my heart. She's such a nice teacher. I don't want her to know that I've been involved in the illegal trafficking of head lice.

She shoves a fist towards me and I step back. She opens the fist, and sitting on her palm is a two dollar coin.

I look at her, confused.

'I really need a few days off,' she says.

'No problem,' Jack says, snatching the two dollars. 'If you just lean in close to Lewis –'

I whack Jack in the arm. 'Why, Miss Norrish? I thought you loved teaching us!'

'Yeah, why would you want to take a day off?' Lewis asks.

'Well . . . for the same reason you would,' she says.

'We're kids,' I say. 'It's our job to try to get days off school by any means necessary. It's in the contract we sign when we're born. But you're supposed to be passionate about education. You're supposed to say things like, "I would do this job even if I wasn't being paid."'

'Well, it's not always easy teaching you guys. If Brent burps the answer to a maths problem one more time . . . And school holidays are nine weeks away. I need a rest.'

I have to break it to her: 'I'm sorry, Miss Norrish, but we can't give you nits.'

'Why not?' she asks.

'Yeah, why not?' Jack asks. 'This is discrimination against teachers.' He jerks his eyes towards the two dollar coin in his grubby little hand.

'You just infected dozens of your peers,' Miss Norrish says. 'I was watching you out of the corner of my eye the whole time. And I demand that you give me nits immediately.'

'But they're just students,' I tell her. 'They don't shower very often and they smell a bit and they have nits half the time anyway. You're a grown woman. Your hair's all shiny and straight, and it smells like daffodils and stuff. I'm sorry. We have standards.'

'Look, I don't have time for this. Here's five dollars,' she says, taking a note from her purse. It's the first note we will have earned.

I look at my business partners to see what they think. Jack's eyes are on fire, but he'd sell one of his grandmother's kidneys for five bucks. Lewis shakes his head to say, *no deal*.

'If you're away we're stuck with Mr Skroop,' I tell her. Deputy Principal Skroop is the Darth Vader of the teaching world. 'And 25 per cent of five dollars just isn't enough for me to risk having Mr Skroop –'

Her hand shoots out towards Lewis's hair to grab some nits. This shocks me. I never saw her as a thief. Lewis pulls his head back just in time.

'This is why I want a few days off! *None of you listen to me!* Either you give me head lice immediately,' she says, her voice now sharp and demanding, 'or I'm afraid I'll be forced to tell Mr Skroop about your shady little head-lice racket.'

I can feel the warmth of the $18.50 in my pocket. I can't give it up.

Jack nudges me and gives me a look that says, *If the lady wants nits, give her nits.*

'Okay,' I say, 'but I don't feel good about this, and I don't want you telling the other teachers.'

Miss Norrish smiles, leans down and

presses her head into the springy blond sponge of Lewis's hair. I can see lice the size of baby cockroaches crawling across the hair bridge from Lewis's scalp onto hers. After ten or 15 seconds I say, 'Okay, that's enough. Consider yourself infected.'

Miss Norrish stands. She waits. She scratches the back of her head near her neck with one long red fingernail. Then on top. Then just above her ear. Within 30 seconds she's scratching all over. She looks relieved.

'Thank you, boys. Not a word of this to anyone . . . or you know what happens?'

We nod.

'Now, off to class.' Miss Norrish turns and disappears around the corner of the hall. Jack kisses the five dollar note.

I know what I have to do. I have no choice. I can't have Skroop as my teacher. What if he wants nits, too?

'Do you mind?' I ask Lewis.

He shrugs.

I take a deep breath and press my head against his. Within seconds I can feel lice scurrying over onto my scalp, beginning to feed, and I start to scratch.

'Hey!' Jack says, outraged. 'Have you paid your two bucks?'

Nit Quiz

I bet you think you know stuff about nits, right? Wrong. Since I almost died in a mutant nit attack*, I've done a bit of research on *pediculus humanus capitis* (their official name), and I'm pretty sure I know more about them than you. Here's a quiz to test how 'nit-smart' you are. This information might, one day, save your life:

1. Even though we call head lice 'nits', which one of these is officially a 'nit'?

   A) Lice eggs

   B) Teenage lice

   C) Grandma lice

   D) Cute little wubbzy baby lice

2. How does a head louse travel?

   A) Jump

   B) Fly

   C) Crawl

   D) None of the above.
   It hoverboards.

3. Head lice are:

A) Arachnids

B) Reptiles

C) Insects

D) Vampires

4. The oldest known head lice specimens were found:

A) About 30 years ago in Gloucestershire, England

B) About 200 years ago in Tanzania, Africa

C) About 10,000 years ago in north-east Brazil

D) One billion years ago on the planet Tralfamadore

WOOHOO! NITS! PAR-TAY!!

5. If you discover that you have head lice you should:

A) Throw a party

B) Run around the house screaming, 'I'm under attack!'

C) Call the fire department

D) Give them to your best friend

E) All of the above

6. The main food source for head lice is:

A) Crispy dandruff chips

B) Human blood

C) Other head lice

D) Cheese sticks

Meanwhile, at Nick's Nit bar . . .

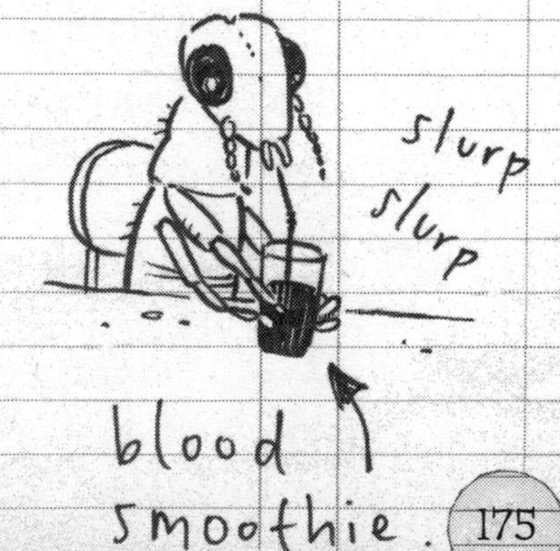

7. Head lice travel at the following speed:

A) About 1.37 centimetres per second

B) About 23 centimetres per minute

C) About 7 metres per hour

D) As fast as the kid carrying them can run

8. The best treatment for getting rid of head lice is:

A) Hair conditioner and comb

B) Peanut butter

C) Picking and eating the lice in a similar manner to a gorilla or chimpanzee

D) Massaging a litre of Neapolitan ice-cream into your scalp and leaving for 30 minutes before rinsing with vinegar

9. True or False: Nits like dirty hair more than they like clean hair.

A) True

B) False

10. The Ancient Egyptians attempted to rid themselves of head lice by:

A) Punching them in the nose

B) Smearing them in mouse fat and reciting an ancient incantation

C) Massaging the scalp with sand

D) Eating warm date meal and water, then spitting it out

Answers:

1) A

2) C

3) C

4) C

5) E

6) B

7) B

8) A – although gorillas and chimpanzees would disagree. Option B works providing you don't have a peanut allergy, and D is unproven yet possibly effective and results in the invention of a new flavour of ice-cream.

9) B

10) D (Option A works well on sharks. Remember that next time you go swimming.)

1–3 Answers Correct: You're a Nitwit. You know so little about nits that you're destined to be infested for the rest of your life.

4–7 Answers Correct: You're a Louse. You know a little but not enough to protect yourself from these bloodthirsty vampires.

8–10 Answers Correct:
Congratulations – you're a Nitologist! You should quit school now and wander the earth spreading your nit knowledge. And your nits.

* To witness me almost dying in a mutant nit attack, read 'Revenge of the Nits', parts one and two, in *My Life & Other Exploding Chickens*.

Runaway Car (Part Two)

I am alone in my grandmother's 1952 Ford Crestline, tearing backwards down Kingsley Street towards the two toughest kids in my class, Brent Bunder and Jonah Flem. I must be doing 60 or 70 kilometres an hour. I'm screaming. They're screaming. There's no way they'll make it out of this alive. I'll be sent to prison for being an underage, unlicensed driver. I'll have to eat sloppy prison food for the rest of my life, and I really don't enjoy sloppy food very much.

I can see their ugly faces through the rear windscreen of the car. In the last seconds of their lives, I try to imagine Brent Bunder and Jonah Flem as a pair of cane toads, like Nan said, so that I won't feel so bad when the car mashes them into the road.

At the very last second, I try jerking the wheel to the right. Brent and Jonah dive to the left onto the gravel at the roadside.

Somehow, I miss them.

I'm so relieved.

'Sorrrryyyy!' I call as I tear past.

'Crazy old lady!' Jonah shouts, throwing a handful of gravel at the car, and I realise he must think Nan's still at the wheel. Then Brent and I make eye contact for a split second.

'You're dead, Weekly!' he screams. Usually having the biggest kid in my school wanting me dead would bother me, but right now it's the least of my worries. If I don't stop this speeding car he won't have the chance to kill me.

I look down and there are three pedals.

I stomp on the one on the right. Nothing happens.

I turn and look out the rear window. While I've been trying to figure out the pedal situation, the car has shot straight past my house and I'm bearing down on the intersection of Kingsley and Tennyson streets. Cars crisscross at high speed from either side of me. I stomp on the left pedal. It's firm and it squeals as I jam my foot down. But the car keeps rolling.

I'm going to hit that concrete truck, I think. I can feel it in my bones. The truck says 'Craig's Concreting' on the side. The truck's rounded tail-end spins. I bang my fist on the horn again and the driver – Craig, I assume – looks up to see Nan's ancient Ford speeding backwards towards him. His mouth forms an 'O' of surprise and he slams on the brakes. His truck squirls and skids 180 degrees so that it, too, is now driving backwards. The slippery dip that the concrete slides out of swings wildly around. Thick, grey goo flies through the air towards Nan's car. It's going to –

Schlump.

The wet concrete hits the top of the car and sprays the side of my face. I'm right behind the truck now as it skids towards me. The numberplate reads 'CON-CR8', and I know it's the last thing that I will ever read because the truck is about to hit my concrete-spattered face.

Prang!

Rip!

Crunch.

The shiny silver bumper bar of Nan's car has been torn off and is now wedged beneath the rear wheels of the concrete truck, which, thankfully, comes to a screaming stop.

The driver shouts something at me and waves his fist, but I don't care. I'm alive!

But not for long.

I look back out the rear window to see the Dog Kisser about to cross the street with nine hounds of varying shapes and sizes on leads. *Oh no.* The Dog Kisser is a weird dog-walking dude in my neighbourhood who loves nothing more than a dog licking him all over the neck, face and mouth. But he might have smooched his last pooch, because I'm about to take the DK and his canine companions out. I stomp on the middle pedal – it has to be the brake – and get ready for the squealing sound of tyres on road.

Nothing happens.

I stomp on the pedal again.

The dogs are looking right at me and barking, but the Dog Kisser, unaware of the car hurtling towards him, is trying to untangle himself from a bunch of leads.

I never liked the DK much. I find it hard to respect a man who has such a high tolerance for canine saliva, but I don't want to make roadkill out of him. I'm five metres from him when I hit the horn. The DK looks up, howls and pulls back hard on the dogs' leads.

The dogs fly through the air towards him.

Whoom!

I zoom past as all nine mutts land on the Dog Kisser and he goes sprawling to the kerb.

'Sorry!' I shout again.

All the dogs start to lick him on the neck and face. It must be the greatest day of his life.

The fire and police stations blur past. Sergeant Hategarden is out front, waxing the bonnet of his police cruiser, holding a large takeaway cup of coffee.

'Heeeeeeeeelp!' I howl.

He looks up, sees Nan's very long, very wide vintage vehicle careering backwards down the street with a child at the wheel. He spills his coffee on his shirt and lunges around the front of the car, into the front seat. I hear the siren start up, but it's too late to save me now.

Kings Bay Swimming Pool is at the end of my street, on the opposite side of the

T-intersection that I'm speeding towards. The road running across is the main street in town, and it's choked with holiday-maker traffic. I'll never get through. Not to worry. It was fun while it lasted. Life, I mean. I had some good times, a few real shockers, but all things must come to an end. I plant my hand firmly on the horn, say my final prayers, secure my seatbelt and get ready for the crash.

Three seconds . . .

A family station wagon with a surfboard on the roof and two bikes on the back crosses the intersection.

Two seconds . . .

A campervan with three long-haired backpackers in the front seat cruises by.

One second . . .

A semitrailer rumbles along in no hurry at all. The truck driver hears my horn and looks up. His eyes go wide. I'm going to miss his cab, but I'm certain to hit the big, heavy trailer that has 'Fielder's Fresh Foods' on the side. I'm going to hit a vegetable truck. What a horrible way to die. Death by pumpkin. I duck down low as my car and his truck collide, and I hear the loudest noise I have ever heard – ripping, tearing, smashing, screeching. The roof of Nan's car is torn off and the rest of the car – with me in it – shoots out from underneath the other side of the truck and across a lane of traffic.

A cyclist coming from my left yells, 'Watch out!' He hits his brakes, flies over the handlebars, slides across the rough, concrete-spattered bonnet and somehow lands on his feet. The back of Nan's car mounts the gutter, tears across the footpath, smashes through the pool fence, knocks over a small palm tree, and cleans up the ice-cream trolley, sending Magnums and Icy Poles flying (but not a single Bubble O' Bill, from what I can see). The car races towards the diving blocks where a row of kids are lining up for a race.

'On your marks . . .' says a voice over the speakers.

The kids turn at the sound of the exploding trolley – there's ice-cream all over my rear windscreen – to see the car hurtling towards them. They dive off the blocks and onto the grass then scramble out of the way, revealing a still, tranquil pool. Nan's car smashes through the diving blocks and goes flying, boot-first, into the deep end, snapping the orange lane ropes. The heavy car begins to sink like the *Titanic*, tipping up at one end.

With me in it.

I'm still above the water, and I suck in an enormous breath before I feel the weight of the back of the car pull me down into the deep. Millions of tiny bubbles roar past me towards the surface.

I can only see white froth. I try to swim up towards the light but the seatbelt holds me down. I reach for my hip and click the release button. The car bangs against the bottom of the pool. I claw at the water, but as I shoot out of the newly convertible car, my shoulder and arm get tangled in the belt. I wrestle with it.

I can't believe my Nan's horrible driving has led to this. All I wanted was a Bubble O' Bill and to go for a swim. At least I got one wish, I guess.

I pull hard and twist my arm out of the belt. I place a foot on the car seat and push upwards, firing like a rocket through a storm of bubbles. I blow air out until I have no more air to blow, but I'm still beneath the surface. I kick and paddle hard, making a desperate squeaking noise as my lungs strain for air. I'm pretty sure I'm going to faint. Then – *schploosh* – I break the surface of the water and drink in the sweet, chlorinated air. There is screaming and cheering all around.

I tread water, wipe my eyes and look to the side of the pool. I bob on the surface, surrounded by thousands of soggy phone book pages. The edge of the pool is lined with kids and parents and pool-workers. An arm wraps around my waist as a guy in a red-and-yellow lifesaver's cap swims me to safety. He boosts me up and out, and I lie flat on the warm tiles.

I am happy to be alive.

'What in God's name are you doing driving a car, boy?' a voice demands.

I open my eyes and sunshine spears them. I squint, still heaving for air, and I make out the face of Sergeant John Hategarden.

'I just wanted an ice-cream,' I say. 'A Bubble O' Bill.'

After the pool's first-aid guy checks me out, Sergeant Hategarden gives me a ride in the police cruiser up to Papa Bear's. Nan is standing outside, looking confused, wondering where her car is.

Hategarden guides her into the back seat alongside me and takes us down to the station. In the interrogation room he informs her: 'You are never allowed to drive again, Nancy.'

'Why?' she asks, surprised.

'Because you don't have a *licence*.'

'Oh, poppycock,' she says. 'I'm an excellent driver. I've been driving since I was seven years old.'

'If you ever drive another vehicle again, even so much as a scooter, you're going to go to jail,' he says, stone-faced.

'What did *I* do? Everything turned out okay in the end. Apart from that blasted semitrailer driver who ripped the roof off my car. He'll pay for that.'

'Nancy, your car is at the bottom of the municipal swimming pool.'

'I'll never get the rust out,' she says.

Hategarden firmly smoothes down the sides of his moustache. 'You're lucky that car didn't kill someone. Do you know it hasn't been registered since 1979?'

'Rules, rules,' she says. 'Life's no fun anymore.'

'You nearly killed your grandson!'

She looks at me. 'You're alright, aren't you, mate? He's a tough little fella, this one. Sergeant, if you could please have my car removed from the swimming pool, we'll be on our way.'

Hategarden lets out a low animal growl of frustration.

'There's no need to be a bear about it,' Nan says. 'You'll give an old lady a fright. Come on,

Tom, let's go get that ice-cream. And maybe we'll go car shopping. I agree with all of you – I think it's time I applied for my licence.'

Acknowledgements

It's a great time to be a writer because readers have a chance to contribute to my stories. While I'm working on a book I visit lots of schools and festivals and libraries. I share one of the stories I'm working on and brainstorm ideas for those stories with lots of super-creative kids. Sometimes those ideas find their way into the book, so here is my thank-you list to all the fantastic kids and teachers who have contributed to this book and have given me feedback on what's working and what could be better.

Special thanks to Luca Bancks for being my first reader and sounding board, and for being so enthusiastic about Tom Weekly's ongoing adventures. And to Amber and Hux for their unrelenting support for my creative work and for blocking their ears when they overhear me reading the particularly disgusting bits.

Big thanks to Anjali Dutton, who wrote the story 'Toffee' when she was 11 years old and won the NSW Pilot PEN short story competition, judged by Andy Griffiths. Anjali rewrote the story for publication in this book. She's such a talented writer, and 'Toffee' will hopefully inspire you to write your own stories!

Thanks to students in the following schools for bainstorming stories with me in live talks and online: Varsity College year 7, Pembroke Junior School, Grand Avenue SS year 4, Hillcrest Christian College years 5 and 6, Scotch College class 5D, St Stephen's and St Imogen, Youngtown PS, Ravenswood PS, Scottsdale PS, Penleigh and Essendon Grammar School year 4, The Southport School, The Pocket PS, All Hallows CPS, Rosary School Adelaide, Coorabell PS year 5/6, Kyogle PS 5/6T, Lismore PS, Mullumbimby PS, Bangalow PS, Modanville PS, Eureka PS, Ivanhoe Girls' Grammar year 3/4, Genesis Christian College, Whitsunday Anglican School, Eagle Junction SS, Kimberley Park SS, Craigslea SS, Blackbutt SS, Everton Park SS, Taranganba SS, Mt Carmel School, The Willows SS, Xavier Catholic College, St Andrew's Catholic College Cairns, St Patrick's School Emerald, Wentworth Falls PS, Gordon East PS, St Ignatius' College Riverview, Albany Creek SS, St Eugene College, Macgregor SS, St Peter's Rochedale, Windsor SS, Brisbane Boys' College, Bray Park SS, Churchie and St Pius

X College, as well as participants in my Brisbane Writers Festival 2016 sessions.

And thanks to the following individuals: Ben, Tina, Harrison, Jackson, Amber, Gideon, Isaac, Caitlin, Dakota, Anthony, Ruby, Gabriella, Nick, Boris, Raph, Zayneb, Lucy, Briannon, Amelie, Sam, Klaes, Joel, Emily, Liam, Sinead, Rex, Finley, Ashwin, Mitch, Josie, Oskar, Fletcher, Matilda, Asia, Eva, Lochie, Bron, Will, Tara, Katie, Suneha, Jem, Connor, Anesa, Erin, Adelia, Elijah, Caleb, Claire, George, Emile, Tom, Noah, Thomas, Nicole, Mitchell, Ashley, Matthew, Aden, Imogen, Indira, Huxley, Luca, Jack, Millie, Gem, Cosmo, Iggy, Maggie, Sol, Bella, Angus and Caleb. And to Tom Kirk for sending me a brilliant 'What Would You Rather Do?' challenge.

Thanks to all the brilliant booksellers, teachers, librarians and parents who share my crazy stories with kids.

Thanks to Gus Gordon for being an all-round nice guy and for bringing Tom Weekly's weird little world to life in pictures. Thanks to the fantastic Anthony Blair and Jo Butler at Cameron's for being a constant source of energy and support, and to the team at Penguin Random House

Australia. Zoe Walton and Brandon VanOver offer up lots of brilliant ideas and push and prod me to make the stories funnier and more detailed. Dot Tonkin, Zoe Bechara, Angela Duke and Suzannah Katris take the books to the world in fun and innovative ways, and Laura Harris and Julie Burland run a super-dynamic team. I feel lucky to be working with you.

May you be well and happy.

Tristan Bancks is a children's and teen author with a background in acting and filmmaking. His books include the *My Life* series, *Mac Slater* (Australia and US) and *Two Wolves* (*On the Run* in the US), a crime-mystery novel for middle-graders. *Two Wolves* won Honour Book in the 2015 Children's Book Council of Australia Book of the Year Awards and was shortlisted for the Prime Minister's Literary Awards. It also won the YABBA and KOALA Children's Choice Awards. His new novel, *The Fall*, is available from May 2017. Tristan is a writer–ambassador for the literacy charity Room to Read. He is excited by the future of storytelling and inspiring others to create.

Gus Gordon has written and illustrated over 70 books for children. He writes books about motorbike-riding stunt chickens, dogs that live in trees, and singing on rooftops in New York. His picture book *Herman and Rosie* was a 2013 CBCA Honour Book. Gus loves speaking to kids about illustration, character design and the desire to control a wiggly line. Visit Gus at www.gusgordon.com

About Tristan Bancks and Room to Read

Tristan Bancks is a committed writer–ambassador for Room to Read, an innovative global non-profit that has impacted the lives of over ten million children in ten low-income countries through its Literacy and Girls' Education programs. Room to Read is changing children's lives in Bangladesh, Cambodia, India, Laos, Nepal, South Africa, Sri Lanka, Tanzania, Vietnam and Zambia – and you can help!

In 2012 Tristan started the Room to Read World Change Challenge in collaboration with Australian school children to build a school library in Siem Reap, Cambodia. Over the years since Tristan, his fellow writer–ambassadors and kids in both Australia and Hong Kong have raised $80,000 to buy 80,000 books for children in low-income countries.

For more information or to join this year's World Change Challenge, visit http://www.tristanbancks.com/p/change-world.html, and to find out more about Room to Read, visit www.roomtoread.org.